# Healing Tides

## A Katama Bay Series

Katie Winters

D1596137

# Chapter One

ONE YEAR EARLIER

Elsa had long ago discovered the truth of parenting. Her children's pain was something colossal; it took a heavy toll on Elsa's psyche, on her soul. As she stood alongside her daughter on that fateful night in mid-June, her daughter's face contorted and twisted; it flashed red and white and filled with sweat and terror. Long ago, Elsa had given birth to her beautiful daughter, and now, this beautiful woman brought another creature into the world — a screaming, vibrant little boy. A little boy who seemed to encompass everything that life was messy, glorious, and mysterious.

The nurses rushed the baby off for a moment. Elsa watched the horror of this play out over her daughter's face. For the previous nine months, Mallory had grown this baby in her belly. She had prayed for good health, ached for him, and dreamed of his future. Now, they'd just taken him away as though none of that mattered. Mallory's eyes found Elsa's, and she squeezed her hand hard.

"You did amazing, Mallory." Elsa's voice broke as she said it. "You're a mommy, now. You brought that baby into the world. And he's going to love you so much."

The wait was excruciating, although it wasn't so long before the baby was returned to Mallory, and she held him, bright-eyed and amazed at the little being in her arms. She whispered to him tenderly, "Hi, honey," over and over again, as though she'd lost all knowledge of any other words. Her fiancé, Lucas, stood on the other side of the hospital bed — just a young adult, twenty-one years old, in awe. All the color had drained from his cheeks as he realized that, yes, this was his son that he helped create—an extension of him that would be for the rest of his life. He was a father, now.

Elsa stepped out of the hospital room to give the new family of three some time alone. Once out in the whitewashed hallway, she glanced up at the clock with tired eyes when she realized just how long her daughter had been in labor. Thirteen hours! It was now five thirty in the morning, and the sun had begun to peek its head from the horizon line. She stepped into the cool breeze of the early morning and closed her eyes. Her heartbeat was steady, somber, and the blood rushed through her ears, a constant reminder that she remained alive—that she was still here.

Elsa lifted her phone from her pocket to find several messages from her husband, Aiden.

> AIDEN: I have to say. I'm so apprehensive. I wish I could be there.
>
> AIDEN: Love you all so much.

Elsa typed back a quick response, although she knew Aiden was assuredly fast asleep. He required so much of it these days.

His body was preparing to rest forever. It was like it wanted a head start.

Elsa returned to the waiting room, where she found her other son and daughter: Cole and Alexie. Twenty-two-year-old Alexie lived in New York and attended NYU but had returned home the previous week due to the occasion. She was zonked out with her long legs stretched out before her and her head tossed back with her long brown locks splayed out every which way. Beside her was Elsa's eldest, Cole, who was twenty-five, stared at his phone despondently.

"Hey, you two. Guess what? You're officially an aunt and an uncle."

Cole jabbed Alexie's shoulder, and Alexie startled from the chair, grumbling at her brother.

"When can we see her?" Alexie asked as she tried to compose herself.

"I think you'll be able to pretty soon. They'll just need to rest for a little while."

"Did you tell her she took long enough?" Cole asked with a cheeky grin.

"Be careful about what you say to her. She's exhausted, and if she murders you? I won't blame her," Elsa teased as she adjusted her purse on her shoulder. "I'm just going to go pick up your dad."

Cole and Alexie exchanged glances as their faces fell.

"Are you sure about that, Mom?" Cole asked.

It was true that in recent days, Aiden had grown into even more of a shell of his previous self. His skeleton had begun to protrude from his skin, and his coloring was all off. Still, that light remained in his eyes, the light Elsa remembered from long ago when she had first fallen for him. At the time, she told her friends that it was as though time had stopped in its tracks.

"Of course I am. Your father is a grandfather for the first time. He can't miss this."

Elsa felt resolute. She clenched the steering wheel somberly as she drove the familiar route from the hospital, south toward Katama Beach, on the southernmost and easternmost tip of Martha's Vineyard. It seemed almost a crime that it was summer. Summer on Martha's Vineyard always seemed to flourish with glorious blue skies, vibrant parties, and soft, white sands and frothy waves; it was laughter with sunshine and never-ending days.

It was also, unfortunately, the time in which Elsa would be forced to say goodbye to the only love she'd ever known.

Elsa parked outside of her house. Her father's vehicle was in her driveway, as was her stepmother's. When she'd left the house the previous day with news of Mallory's labor, Nancy had been the only one around. But this was just like Elsa's father, Neal. He didn't like to be away from Nancy for long.

Neal and Nancy were both early risers. When Elsa stepped into the foyer, she spotted them both at the kitchen table, cozied up in two of the fluffy robes they'd taken from Katama Lodge and Wellness Spa, the business that Neal had opened himself and managed for years.

"Well, look what the cat dragged in!" Nancy's sweet voice swirled from the kitchen. She leaped to her feet, an incredibly spry woman of fifty-eight, and beamed as Elsa entered. "Has it happened? Do we have a new great-grandbaby?"

Elsa returned her smile. "We do. Mallory did a fantastic job. Both Mom and baby are resting."

"Incredible," Neal beamed. "I knew that girl could do anything."

Neal stood to hug Elsa next, then stepped back to pour her a mug of coffee. Elsa watched her father's strong back and large, capable hands as he selected a mug. Ever since she'd been a little girl, she had always adored her father. Some small, scared part of herself longed to fall into his arms and cry.

How was it possible that she was already a grandmother?

How was it possible that her husband was on the verge of death? How had any of this happened?

And still, she was meant to be so grateful. And she was! How strange and how honored she was to have been allowed such love in her life.

Her father's eyes were somber when he turned back. Elsa swallowed the lump in her throat as she took the mug.

"He slept peacefully last night," Neal said finally. "We told him to call us if he needed anything."

"You know, he wouldn't want to bother us if he didn't really have to," Nancy pointed out. "He's not the kind of man to complain."

"I think I'm going to bring him to the hospital," Elsa said.

Nancy and Neal exchanged glances; their looks were similar to what Cole and Alexie had worn.

"Are you sure that's a good idea?" Neal finally asked.

"He needs to meet his grandson," Elsa replied with firmness in her voice. "And I know he can do it. I'll bring the wheelchair. He doesn't want to live out his last days in that room. You know Aiden. We all do."

Elsa sipped the rest of her coffee. Neal grimaced, then said, "Okay. But I'm driving you up in the van."

"Dad, you don't have to do that."

"I insist. Besides, we want to meet the baby, too. That's my great-grandchild."

Elsa appeared in the dark shadows of the bedroom they'd set up for Aiden after he had been released from the hospital. Treatment hadn't worked at all; the cancer had metastasized from his prostate, and they simply hadn't caught it in time. Elsa could pinpoint a number of things to blame. Over the years, Aiden had worked terrifically hard at his job as a stockbroker, and in his free time, he had given everything to his family. His health had always been stellar; he'd always been strong, fast and lithe. He'd been a successful sailor and a terrific swimmer.

5

---

He had even dabbled in tennis and weight lifting. His body had seemed an extension of his personality: vibrant, alive.

And now, it had failed him.

Elsa hesitated for a moment. She wasn't entirely sure she should wake him. And always, in these moments before she did wake him, she worried that, in fact, she wouldn't be able to. Had she already missed her "goodbye"?

As though his dream-self could hear her, Aiden's eyes suddenly flickered open. He coughed twice, then whispered, "Is that my girl?" His voice was hardly audible.

Elsa stepped forward hurriedly and placed her hand over his. Her heart leaped into her throat. "Hi, baby. How are you feeling?"

Aiden blinked several times. It seemed to take him more and more time to return to the world, but he smiled and nodded, indicating he was okay.

"Did she do it? Is our girl a mother?" He managed to ask.

"She is."

"Wow. I can't believe it." He shook his head slightly across the pillow. "You always think about these huge moments in your life, you know? Guess I didn't imagine it like this."

Elsa's throat constricted. "I'm taking you there. If you think you're up for it."

Aiden's eyes widened. After a long pause, he nodded. "It's the only place in the world I want to be."

It took a bit of time to prepare. Elsa helped Aiden get dressed, then watched as her father assisted him into his wheelchair. Neal, being a much older man, should not have been so much stronger than her once healthy and powerful husband. It was heartbreaking to watch.

But gosh, was she grateful for him just then, or what.

They drove in the Katama Lodge van all the way back to the hospital. They were silent, save for one phone call that Neal made to the Katama Lodge about an incident with one of their current residents. This celebrity woman apparently wasn't happy with the comfort level of her bed. Elsa wanted to laugh aloud at the atrocious behavior of such people, but she literally didn't have the strength. Today was all about her daughter, Mallory, and their new grandchild.

Elsa wheeled her husband through the glossy white halls of the hospital, all the way to Mallory's room. The room was drenched in the morning light, and it seemed like a portal to heaven. Their daughter was fast asleep. Her lips were closed, and her skin was dewy and beautiful; she herself looked like an angel lying there so peacefully.

Lucas was nowhere to be found, and Elsa was grateful for this. She loved Lucas, but she just wanted some private moments with her husband and grandchild, whose eyes were closed. His eyelids were almost translucent. He lay there sleeping peacefully without a single movement other than his chest falling up and down from his light breathing. Elsa stepped toward the bassinet; she was hardly able to breathe.

Aiden wheeled himself closer and peered in alongside her. He shook his head delicately. "I can't believe it," he said. "I was so worried I wouldn't be able to meet him. He's beautiful."

The words felt like a knife. Elsa forced herself not to react.

Elsa helped draw the baby from the bassinet and place him in her husband's arms. She cursed the tears that trickled from the sides of her eyes. How dare they blur this moment— a moment she wanted to remember for the rest of her life.

"Hi, little guy," Aiden whispered. "Look at you. You're already so strong, aren't you? You're going to make your mom crazy. She's going to love you to pieces."

Elsa's hands shook as she lifted her phone to take several photos of the scene: her husband, bald, his cheeks hollow and weak from chemo, holding his grandson, who still didn't have a name.

Aiden's eyes returned to hers as the baby slept in his arms. "Thank you for this, Elsa."

Elsa furrowed her brow. She didn't want these conversations. She didn't want him to acknowledge just how difficult this was.

"Seriously," he continued. "This is the best gift you could have given me."

"He's your grandson. Of course, you deserve to meet him."

Aiden nodded. "I know. But I just want you to know that this and every single moment of my life with you has been extraordinary. I've loved every moment. When I met you, I knew you would change my life. But I couldn't have even imagined how beautiful it would be."

Elsa's nostrils flared. She crossed and uncrossed her arms. She felt like a child that needed to have a tantrum. She wanted to stomp her foot and scream to God above that it wasn't over yet. It couldn't be over; how on earth could this possibly be it? She was only forty-four-years-old and Aiden was only fifty-one.

"I love you, too," were the words she was able to muster in return. They seemed so inadequate at that moment when compared to everything else. As her eyes brewed with more tears, she said, "I love you so much that it might kill me."

Aiden laughed and shook his head sadly. "Don't let it. If anything, I want your love to help you keep living. You have so much of it. And you need to stick around for Mallory, Cole, and Alexie. And now for this little guy, whoever he turns out to be."

Elsa nodded as she felt the tears roll down her cheeks. She swallowed the lump in her throat and silently watched the love of her life hold their first grandchild. She thought about how beautiful life could be one minute and so unfair the next.

# Chapter Two

SIX MONTHS AFTER AIDEN'S DEATH

Baby Zachery kicked his little feet at the base of his baby carrier and cooed up at Elsa. Her black dress, the one she had picked out for Aiden's funeral six months earlier, no longer fit her properly; it hung on her shoulders as though she was an improperly-made mannequin, on the verge of becoming a skeleton in a science exhibition. She bent down and adjusted Zachery's pacifier, which he had spit out of his little mouth. On the right-hand side of his chest was a little stain from the mashed peas she'd fed him earlier. She would have to change him before the funeral.

A shadow danced from the doorway. Elsa turned to glance up at Nancy, who wore a similar black dress. She adjusted an earring in her right ear and tried, then failed, to give Elsa a smile. Now that Elsa's father had passed away, they were both widows. They had to be one another's backbones and pick one another up when they fell.

It seemed ridiculous that so much tragedy and pain had happened within the past six months. It seemed crazy that Elsa had to say goodbye to her father so soon after she'd said goodbye to her husband, Aiden. Maybe it was all a dream, a nightmare she would soon rise from. Perhaps she would turn into Aiden's big, strong arms and whisper, *"That was a horrible dream,"* and he would whisper, *"Try to go back to sleep. Things will be all right in the morning."*

"Are you ready, honey?" Nancy asked. "I want to get to the funeral home a little early."

"Of course," Elsa replied and reached for another of Zachery's baby onesies. "I just need to change him quick. Mallory will meet us up there. I think she gets off work at two."

"So nice of you to babysit," Nancy offered.

Elsa wanted to correct her stepmother. In truth, babysitting Zachery was the only thing that kept the pieces of her soul intact. More than anything, she loved baby Zachery with every ounce in her. He looked at her with love and happiness, not knowing what was happening around them. Certainly, not the way so many other islanders cast pity her way. It wasn't that she blamed them. After all, she'd lost her husband and then, almost immediately afterward, her father in the span of just over six months. She might have pitied her, too.

Nancy continued to hover in the doorway while Elsa changed the baby. It was strangely silent in the large house— the Katama Beach home where Elsa had spent the first eighteen years of her life. In the wake of Aiden's death, she had moved back. She couldn't return to the house she had raised her two children in, the house she had so many wonderful memories in, or shared with her late husband because it was just too painful and fresh.

"I've been thinking," Nancy began gently. "I've been thinking a lot about the Lodge."

Elsa bristled at the thought of work. Since her father's rather unexpected passing, they'd stopped taking appointments and had told everyone en route for their stays at the Lodge to remain home. Their second-in-command now looked over the women who'd already been on-site. Soon, the place would be dismal and empty.

"What about the Lodge?" Elsa finally asked as Zachery cooed his own opinion below.

"I just don't know if we should reopen right away," Nancy said. "I'm not sure how we could even manage it. Not without your father."

Elsa nodded somberly. "I've been thinking the same thing. It just terrifies me, not having it in my life."

"I know." Nancy exhaled drearily. "It's been my home for ten years. It gave me new life after... well."

Elsa knew quite a bit about Nancy's previous life. She had shared a lot with Elsa about how she had struggled with money and alcohol and had a daughter she no longer spoke to in Manhattan. Neal had helped her heal and become the woman she is today. He had taught her that she was worthy of love, even after so much torment.

"We'll find a way to reopen, maybe. Someday," Elsa murmured as she zipped up Zachery's onesie.

But the concept of "someday" no longer seemed so certain, not after so much had been taken from her.

The funeral home was a one-story building with plum-colored walls and plush rugs that gave the slightest bit when you walked over them. Elsa held the baby on her chest and shifted her weight as Nancy spoke with the funeral home directors about the coming hours of the visitation. Elsa had had a similar conversation with the men six months earlier. It was as though they read from the same script every time, regardless of who had died. She supposed she couldn't blame them for this. They'd probably found a formula and decided to stick to it. Everything had a formula, even saying goodbye.

When Nancy finished her conversation, she stepped back and splayed her hand over Zachery's tender head. "He's being so good," she said, as though she wasn't sure what else to say. "Have you heard from Carmella?"

Elsa made a guttural noise in her throat. She had hardly seen her sister since their father's passing. She'd, of course, called her from the hospital after they had rushed him there and had listened to the silence as her sister had processed the news of his death. Carmella had come to the hospital eventually, but she'd kept a wide berth from everyone. When Nancy had approached her for a tearful hug, Carmella had shed no tears. The woman was cold. She'd always been that way.

"I'm sure she'll make it eventually," Elsa returned as she flared her nostrils. "He was her only dad, after all."

Nancy's lips twisted slightly. Admittedly, Nancy and Carmella had never been particularly close. Carmella had adored her stepmother before Nancy, Karen — a woman who had said some of the cruelest things Elsa had heard in her life. To Aiden, Elsa had referred to Karen as *"my ex-wicked step-mother."* As a contrast, Carmella and Karen had been thick as thieves.

Of course, the minute Neal divorced Karen, Elsa was sure Karen hadn't bothered to keep up with Carmella. She had wondered what Carmella thought about that, and if she felt abandoned at all. But it wasn't like Carmella would ever open up to Elsa about something like that.

Islanders began to arrive just after two. In the first group, Mallory and her fiancé, Lucas, appeared dressed both in black. Mallory's cheeks were already stained black with eyeliner from crying. She took Baby Zachery in her arms as she thanked her mother for babysitting.

"There's already so many people here," she whispered as she eyed the crowd.

"Your grandfather was well-loved across the island," Elsa affirmed.

"People have been stopping me in random places all week, telling me how sorry they are," Mallory said. "At the grocery store and at the gym and at work. It's nice, but it's also over-whelming. It's destroying me. It makes me want to burst into tears every single time."

Elsa rubbed her daughter's upper back as an older gentleman approached her. Elsa recognized him as Wes Sheri-dan, another icon on the island. He owned the Sunrise Cove Inn. As both Neal and Wes had been around the same age and both in the hospitality sector in a general sense, they had been close over the years.

"I'm so sorry for your loss, Elsa," Wes said. His eyes glowed as though he tried to keep his tears at bay. "He was such a great man, your father."

"Thank you, Mr. Sheridan," Elsa replied.

Beside him, Wes's three daughters stood in black dresses. They were each uniquely beautiful, with similar features that manifested wildly different personalities. Elsa had never known them well, but the island knew their names — Susan, Christine, and Lola. They had arrived back to Martha's Vine-yard after years away, and the island had welcomed them back with open arms. Elsa knew that the Sheridan's had experienced their own share of heartaches. Their mother, Anna, had died in a boating accident when the girls had been teenagers. Assuredly, they carried that pain with them always. Elsa knew she would do the same for Aiden, for her mother, and for her younger brother, Colton, and now, again, for her father, Neal.

Elsa and Nancy continued to greet members of the community. Elsa grew fatigued; her eyesight blurred. So many folks seemed to want to talk her ear off about what Neal had meant to them; for whatever reason, she didn't want to hear it. She wanted to toil in her bed alone. She wanted to curl up in a ball and sleep without dreaming.

Just past three, a full hour after the visitation had begun, Carmella sauntered into the funeral home. Elsa felt her presence like a black hole. She wore dark sunglasses and a bohemian black dress with a pair of trendy boots, and her hair hung gloriously down her back as though she was headed for a date rather than her father's funeral. Elsa's eyes burned toward her sister, and Carmella stopped dead toward the far end of the visitation hall.

"I'll be right back," Elsa told Nancy, who was in the middle of a conversation with the woman who owned the flower shop in Oak Bluffs, Claire.

"Where have you been?" Elsa demanded of Carmella in a strange hiss.

Carmella arched her eyebrow and didn't bother to remove her sunglasses. "I'm here now, aren't I?"

"It's not exactly cool to come late to your father's visitation, FYI." Elsa crossed and uncrossed her arms. She was reminded of once when they'd been teenagers when Elsa had caught Carmella sneaking out of the house. Elsa had sounded just like this; cold as ice, older and stiffer.

"Whatever, Elsa. Just let me grieve my father in peace."

"We have to be there for each other," Elsa muttered. The last thing she wanted to do was cause a scene.

"Yeah? The way you were there for me when we were younger? When Mom and Dad were happy to let me rot in my guilt?"

Elsa rolled her eyes back. "You're so dramatic. Dad was nothing but a saint and you know that."

Carmella ripped off her sunglasses at that moment. Her eyes were tinged red. Elsa was taken aback. Maybe she'd half-expected her sister not to even bother to cry.

"Dad loved you to pieces. That's true," Carmella whispered, so low that Elsa had to strain to hear. "But he thought I was secondhand trash, and you know that."

"That's ridiculous," Elsa breathed.

"All these people in this funeral home just loved him. They'd never believe how cold he was to me. And it's not like you paid enough attention to notice."

Elsa's cheeks burned hot. She glanced again toward the front of the visitation room, where her father's coffin shone from the soft light from the hanging lamps.

"This isn't the time or the place for anything like that," Elsa finally hissed back. "And besides, you're forty-one-years-old. Don't you think it's time to grow up? Get over the damn past?"

Little dimples formed in Carmella's cheeks as she smirked. Elsa swam in resentment. She couldn't remember the last time she and her sister had had a pleasant conversation. Even though they were coworkers at the Lodge, they made sure they hardly saw one another by staying in their own space.

"If you'll excuse me, I'd like to go say goodbye to my father," Carmella hissed through her gritted teeth. "I don't mean to bear my truth to you here. I know it's too hard for you to hear."

Carmella brushed past Elsa after that. Elsa turned as her chest caved in. From there in the back, she watched as Carmella stood stone-faced in front of the casket. What was it that Elsa wanted Carmella to do? Did she want her to break down? Did she want her to admit all she'd done wrong?

Years ago, at their mother's funeral, Carmella hadn't cried, either. Elsa had been enraged with her until she had discovered that throughout the ceremony, Carmella had scraped her fingernails across her upper arms so much that she'd bled all over her dress.

But that had all been such a long time ago.

They were adults now. The past was the past. And Elsa knew in her heart that the two of them would never see eye to eye. It was impossible.

# Chapter Three

Present Day

The Katama Lodge and Wellness Spa had been reopened for a full week. Elsa sat at the edge of her desk and blinked through the enormous bay window, which reflected back a picture-perfect view of Katama Bay. She had kicked off her heels, as she'd grown so accustomed to wearing slippers around the house, and her tights strained against her stomach. After all, the sweatpants and jeans she had taken to since the Lodge's closing the previous January had been particularly forgiving, and she'd let herself indulge.

Apparently, the time for all that relaxation, mourning, and the darkness of living in the aftermath of so much horror was meant to be over. The past six weeks had been a whirlwind. Nancy's real daughter, Janine Grimson, had recently arrived from Manhattan after a particularly horrendous situation. Her best friend since childhood had had an affair with her very

17

famous, very rich husband, and news of Janine's "mental collapse" had been all over the tabloids. Nancy had been up in arms in the wake of it. *"Do you think I should write her? I could tell her to come here? Oh gosh, what do you think I should do? I don't know if she could ever forgive me!"* Finally, Nancy had, of course, written her, and Janine had accepted Nancy's invite to stay with her on the island and of course, this had ultimately flipped Elsa's life upside down.

It wasn't that she wasn't happy for Nancy. Nancy had craved a reunion with her daughter since her arrival to the island over a decade ago. It had come up in conversation frequently. Now, here she was: a stepsister Elsa had never really wanted. And somehow, Janine had convinced them all to reopen the Katama Lodge and Wellness Spa.

In some respects, Elsa thought, *how dare she?* After all, it wasn't like Janine knew any of the hardships Elsa and Nancy had been through the previous year. Elsa had lost her husband and then her father. The pain was still so fresh. Sometimes, the thought of putting one foot in front of the other filled her with dread. Now, she had a jam-packed working schedule, overly tight skirts, and a whole host of phone calls to make. The Katama Lodge was back and the world was thrilled about it, regardless of what Elsa's opinion was. All Elsa wanted to do was sleep.

There was a knock on the door. Elsa jumped up, pushed her feet into her heels, then opened the door to find Janine. Janine wore all white; her face was fresh and clean and tanned from her long runs on the island. Her smile was electric and probably the result of some super-expensive, teeth-whitening job up in Manhattan.

"Hi! What's up?" Elsa forced herself to sound upbeat.

"Hey! I just wanted to let you know, Jennifer Conrad is at the front desk. She says she has a meeting with you, but you haven't answered your phone?"

"Shoot." Elsa yanked open the door wider and hustled through the hallway. Jennifer, that red-haired, long-legged beauty, who ran the social media firm in downtown Edgartown, along with her mother's bakery, the Frosted Delights, awaited her, briefcase in hand. "Jennifer! I'm terribly sorry. I left my phone on silent after yoga class. Silly mistake."

Jennifer was easygoing. She waved her hand to and fro and said, "I do that stuff all the time. Don't worry about it."

Elsa could smell the lie, which of course, women like Jennifer Conrad didn't make mistakes like that. Even still, she was grateful for the pass.

"Good to see you again, Jennifer!" Janine said as she hustled past. "I just have another appointment I have to get to. Good luck on the social media strategy!"

"Good to see you too, Janine. Still on for that wine later this week?" Jennifer asked.

"I wouldn't miss it," Janine returned.

Of course, Elsa thought. Janine burst into her world and immediately, Martha's Vineyard took to her with friendliness and love. Meanwhile, Elsa's heart grew darker; her depression cloud was turning into a storm.

"Thank you for coming in today," Elsa said as Jennifer sat across from her. "I've been a bit lax on the social media side of things, and I would love your help. As you know, we've been off the grid for over six months. We need to get back out there."

"Of course," Jennifer returned. "And in fact, I've been in conversation with a number of highly influential social media personalities who would love to spend a night or two here at the Lodge, and you know, show the world what it's like. Like here, we have Debbie Walter. She's forty-two and a popular mommy-blogger, who frequently writes also about the benefits of putting your needs higher up on the list of to-dos, despite having children. She has over a million followers."

Elsa nodded and furrowed her brow purposely as a way to appear interested. In truth, Jennifer's voice grated on her ears.

Jennifer continued on with the meeting, highlighting how she wanted to boost their social media numbers up twenty-five percent over the course of four months. Elsa couldn't help but remember what her father had once said about social media. "It's the garbage dump of our society." Even still, she knew social media was here to stay, the only way forward. She had to play along, especially if she was going to have continued success as the public relations manager at the Lodge.

After Jennifer left, Elsa wandered from the office toward the dining area, where a number of Lodge residents sat in cozy robes and sipped green tea and spoke in low tones about where they'd been, what they'd gone through, and what areas of their lives they wanted to improve. Throughout her career at the Lodge, Elsa had always loved this part the most — helping others kick-start their paths forward.

But she now found that it irritated her a great deal — especially when she heard things like, *"I just couldn't love my husband anymore."* What the heck did that mean? Her husband had died! She still loved him with all her heart and soul and mind. How could you just stop loving someone you had vowed to love forever?

She knew this was her cross to bear, but it seemed to grow heavier by the day.

It was just after two in the afternoon. Elsa's stomach threatened to eat her from the inside, so she stepped into the kitchen to check on the chef, Cynthia, who said she would whip her up a soup and salad combo in no time. Cynthia had worked for the Lodge several years before, and Nancy had had a good idea to ask her back. She was a warm and welcoming woman of just over fifty, slightly overweight — which made you trust her even more, as she worked as a chef. She was trained in all matters of nutrition. She paid attention to the detailed instructions lent to her by Janine, often concocting entire meals for specific patients based on their needs.

"You look a bit tired, Elsa," Cynthia commented as she sliced through a red onion. "Are you sleeping all right?"

In truth, Elsa hadn't slept properly in well over two years since Aiden's diagnosis and the beginning of her own personal hell on earth.

"Oh, just fine. I forgot how difficult it is to keep up with everything at the Lodge. That's all."

Cynthia arched an eyebrow as she fluffed several spinach leaves into a large bowl. "I have to say. I like that Janine. She's a wonderful part of the new Lodge. Suppose I shouldn't be too surprised since she's Nancy's daughter."

Elsa made a small noise in her throat. At that moment, Janine whipped past the window between the kitchen and the greater dining room. She paused at a table and placed a gentle hand on the top of another woman's shoulder as she pointed out something on her nutritional chart. Janine very much gave off the air of genuine kindness; nobody was an afterthought.

But of course, Janine was no Neal Remington. Nobody was.

"Not to say that your father isn't dearly missed," Cynthia said hurriedly, as though she could sense the words as they spun through Elsa's mind.

Elsa took her salad and soup to her office, where she ate somberly and gazed out at the water. Something was horrific about feeding herself in the midst of a depressive episode. Something in the back of her skull demanded of her, *why do we keep doing this? Why must we keep ourselves going like this? What's the point?*

Another rap sounded on the door. Elsa called, "Come in!" and Nancy rushed in, her smile electric.

"There you are."

"Yep." Elsa placed her fork in her salad bowl and blinked at her stepmother, the woman she had loved so dearly over the past ten-plus years. She felt childish in her resentment. She needed to fix it. "What's going on?"

"Oh, I wanted to let you know that we're having a bit of an incident. Carmella got into a little spat with one of the guests."

Elsa's nostrils flared. "What happened?"

Nancy strung her fingers through her hair. "It's not a big deal. The woman wasn't even one of Carmella's acupuncture patients. Apparently, she was very rude to Carmella at the front desk and insinuated she was some kind of secretary. You know how Carmella bristles at any sign of lack of — shall we say, respect..."

"I've told her over and over again. She has to think of the guests first," Elsa muttered. "Gosh, she can make a mess like nobody's business. She was the one who wanted to reopen the Lodge so bad! And this is how she handles it?"

"I offered the woman several free massages and yoga sessions," Nancy continued. "Carmella's calmed down, thank goodness."

"We're supposed to be a place of calm and relaxation," Elsa said. She stood, her soup untouched, and pointed herself toward the door. "I have to talk to her."

Nancy shifted her weight. "Really. I just wanted to let you know in case you get a complaint on social media or through email. This is not a big deal. The woman has been handled. I think she had her panties in a knot, too."

Elsa's heart sped up. It was like a butterfly, fluttering around her rib cage. Nancy's brow furrowed even more.

"Elsa. Are you okay?" She sounded suddenly terrified.

The room began to spin. Elsa gripped either side of her chair and returned to it. She blinked as her equilibrium returned.

"I'm fine." She heard herself say, although her voice sounded very far away. "Really, I'm good."

Nancy remained over her desk for a moment. "You're going to eat the rest of that soup, right?"

Elsa nodded.

"Okay." Nancy crossed and uncrossed her arms. "I hope this isn't too much for you right now. I know it's a lot, getting back in the saddle, especially without Neal around. If you want, we can hire someone else to help out with some of the things you handle."

"No. It's not necessary," Elsa told her. "Really." She forced herself to smile. "You know how I am."

"Your dad always did say you could handle anything," Nancy returned. "But remember. Even superheroes have to eat lunch." She lifted her wrist to check her watch after that, then nodded. "Okay. Well, I have another appointment. See you later tonight? Janine suggested takeout from the Mexican place."

When Nancy disappeared again, Elsa lifted her chin toward the sky. Her heart continued to hammer in her chest strangely.

"Dad. I don't know how I can do any of this without you," she breathed. "Will you give me some kind of strength to keep going?" Tears rolled down her cheeks and left streaks down her face. She had never felt so alone before in her entire life.

# Chapter Four

For many months after Aiden's death, Elsa struggled to remember not to return home. Her autopilot kicked in as she rushed down Katama Road, headed for the four-bedroom haven she and Aiden had selected together all those years ago. Their cozy kitchen with its yellow paint and its fluttering lace curtains and the massive couch upon which she'd found Aiden fast asleep probably over a thousand times. Sometimes, she made the drive all the way and then hovered in the driveway as tears rushed down her cheeks. Her stomach quaked with a single answer: if she entered that house, she would fall on the floor and be unable to leave it.

Her return to her childhood home was more automatic now that it was July of the following year. Her heart no longer screamed, expecting to see her father's face, either. It was as though her brain had closed off several of its emotional sectors so that she was able to get through the healthy mechanisms of her everyday life. She supposed this was how the body waged war on sadness. It was how anyone could really cope with anything, even in the worst of times.

Elsa stepped into the cool shadows of the house, placed her purse near the foyer table, and stepped into the hallway between the foyer and the yonder kitchen. The large door between the kitchen and the back porch was open to allow the fresh sea breeze to waft through, and she closed her eyes for a moment to inhale, exhale. The sound of the waves was nourishing. It seemed to lift her from the ground the slightest bit.

"I remember that!" Nancy's voice rang out as she burst into laughter. Immediately after, Janine's laughter rollicked, as well.

Throughout the first several weeks of Janine's stay at the house, Elsa hadn't heard Janine laugh even once. She had been a shell of a person who had hardly managed to look Nancy in the eye. Now, it seemed, their routine was to take a bottle of wine to the porch as their conversation danced around old memories. This made Elsa long for peace that much more.

But unfortunately, Nancy had heard her come in.

"Elsa? Is that you?" Nancy's shadow appeared on the other side of the screen door. The door flashed open to reveal her, sun-tanned and healthy, her hair windswept. "Goodness, I thought you'd never get home! Janine and I just opened some Pinot. Let me get you a glass."

Elsa grimaced. She felt like a stranger in her childhood home. There was the quick creak, then slam of one of the cabinet doors, and then, Nancy reappeared in the doorway, gesturing for Elsa to come along. "The light is perfect right now. Come and relax with us."

Elsa walked like a zombie toward the back porch. Nancy's smile was welcoming, even as her eyes told a story of confusion and worry.

"Are you feeling okay? Did you manage to eat the rest of that soup?"

"Yes." This, of course, was a lie. She hovered toward the side of the porch and watched as Nancy filled her glass.

Janine wore a pair of cream linen pants and a tank top that

highlighted her perfectly sculpted shoulders. Her smile was electric. Elsa had a flashing memory of seeing that very smile on the cover of a tabloid magazine, one of the first days she had fully realized the extent of what had happened to Janine over in Manhattan. **SOCIALITE FINDS HUSBAND WITH BEST FRIEND** had been the headline.

Elsa had marveled at how any man could treat such a beautiful woman like garbage.

"I hardly saw you today," Janine said. "Everything go okay with Jennifer?"

Elsa blinked twice before the memory of her meeting with Jennifer came back. "Yes. She really knows what she's talking about." She paused, recognized that Janine wanted more from her, then added, "I can't really keep up with all this social media stuff. It's like the rules of the game change every five minutes."

"I know exactly what you mean," Janine agreed. "My daughters try to keep me in the loop. I recently asked Maggie, 'What is this new video one? With all these dance videos?' and I could practically see her eyes roll back in her head as she tried to answer."

Elsa's laugh sounded false. Janine shook one of the chairs out from beneath the table and gestured. "Come on! Sit with us. I have fresh watermelon in the fridge, and Mom was just talking about making breadsticks, although I told her that's a dangerous game."

Elsa sat with her glass of wine and tried her best to deliver a sterling smile. Nancy's and Janine's eyes returned to one another. They'd dealt with the "Elsa situation," and now, they could return to their newly bubbling relationship.

"Oh, but you must remember that older man who worked at that bodega in Williamsburg," Nancy said as she snapped her fingers. "The one who walked with a cane and had that tabby cat on his shoulder all the time?"

"I do! Rex! He always gave me a piece of candy when we went in there. And he always asked if you wanted him to adopt you," Janine returned.

Nancy's eyes closed as her smile flourished. "He was one of the kindest old men. You must have been six or seven, so I was only..."

"Twenty-two or so?" Janine chimed in.

"That's right. It's hard to believe it."

"We were both such babies," Janine said. "Oh, and remember some of the schemes you got us into? That guy asked you to sell all those knockoff purses on the sidewalk outside that department store."

Nancy smacked her palm across her thigh. "I can't believe you remember that! You were really little then. I think maybe five?"

"Yes, but I remember those purses, especially how they smelled. Like burning plastic." Janine scrunched her nose.

"You sold knockoff purses? On the street?" Elsa tried her best to fall into conversation. Maybe any sign of life from her would make her feel more human, if only to herself.

Nancy and Janine nodded half-heartedly as Nancy said, "I was such an idiot back then. I did anything to try to keep food on the table."

Elsa's heart dropped. She'd known this element of Nancy's life, absolutely. However, it was still difficult for her to fully imagine it, especially since she'd met Nancy within the context of her father's life. Her father had always been one-hundred-percent perfect and a stand-up citizen.

"Oh, I'm so glad your father never learned about those knockoff purses," Nancy said then with a rumbling laugh. "He was such an upstanding citizen."

"Come on. He was a man of industry," Janine returned. "The people demanded knockoff purses, and you were there to sell them."

Elsa arched an eyebrow. "Once, when I was a little girl, I accidentally stole a pack of gum from the gas station. Dad found out about it and made me return it with a letter of apology."

Janine's smile faltered. She turned her eyes toward her glass of wine. Elsa felt her cheeks grow warm. Perhaps she shouldn't have said that. Probably, Janine thought she was comparing her own life with Janine and Nancy's previous one. It was as though she had said, *Oh, well, in this house, we didn't break the law.* But wasn't that the truth?

"Well, I'm pretty sure I stole gum all the time," Janine said mischievously.

"You were a Brooklyn baby. It was just how you got by," Nancy returned.

"Yes. Maxine and I had an entire system," Janine returned. "Oh, but I probably shouldn't say anything like that around you, Elsa. I'm starting to feel like a bad kid."

Nancy and Janine burst into another round of laughter as Nancy traced their path toward yet another story. Elsa sipped her wine and gazed out across the waves. The beach was all theirs for nearly a mile, white and somber and terribly deserted. At the far end, a seagull jumped on land, toward the water, with his beak lifted. Why was it that birds spent any time at all on land? Did they not understand what a privilege it was to fly?

That moment, the front door creaked open. There was the sound of a baby's wail — a baby Elsa knew well. She leaped up as Nancy called, "Is that baby Zachery I hear?"

Elsa drew open the screen door and discovered her daughter, Mallory, with the baby carrier in tow. Her daughter's shoulders were slumped forward, her cheeks were hollowed out, and her eyes reflected chaotic inner storms and loneliness. Elsa remembered her first years of motherhood. How exhausting and demanding it was. Also, regardless of the immensity of your love, you never felt like enough.

"Honey, I didn't know you were coming by." Elsa forced her voice to brighten as she rushed toward her.

Mallory placed Zachery's carrier on the floor and then lifted her hands to her elbows to cup them. Her chin quivered, just as it had when she'd been a child.

"Are you okay?" Elsa whispered. She wrapped her arms around Mallory and placed her hand delicately over the back of her head. Mallory shook against her as Zachery kicked his legs and sucked on his pacifier below them.

"Can we go for a drive?" Mallory exhaled.

In minutes, they'd strapped the baby carrier into the back of Elsa's car. Mallory's knees clacked together as she buckled her seat belt and whipped her long curls over her shoulder. As Elsa backed down the driveway, her eyes caught the slight slant of Mallory's nose, which always reminded her of Aiden.

Elsa drove west, toward the Aquinnah Cliffs Overlook, with its immense white cliffs and glorious view of the sea below. Mallory hiccupped twice as tears rolled down her cheeks. Elsa knew better than to ask what was wrong. Mallory would tell her when she felt strong enough.

Finally, Elsa cut the engine in the lot nearest the overlooks. Mallory turned back to gaze at Zachery, who'd fallen asleep. The silence felt heavy and thick.

"We couldn't get him to stop crying all night," Mallory breathed. "It was awful. Lucas needs to sleep for work. It's been so busy at the docks, and you know, he has to get there before the sun comes up, so it's pretty intense. But it's not like I don't have work, too. And sometimes, we argue about it. About who should get more sleep. About who deserves it more. And the arguments have gotten really crazy lately."

Elsa had noticed the slight tension between Mallory and Lucas the last time they'd eaten lunch together. Mallory had swatted his hand away when he'd tried to hold hers. Elsa had worried but prayed that it was just an ordinary spat between two new parents.

"It's gotten so hard lately. To feel anything for him," Mallory continued. She didn't turn her eyes toward her mother as though shame forced her to look elsewhere. "And we don't have any time for one another. It's like we see each other as potential babysitters, and that's it. And of course, because I'm the mom, most of that work falls on me. It's like we're supposed to live in this modern society, right? But still, when Zach starts to cry, Lucas just rolls over in bed and places his pillow over his head."

Elsa's nostrils flared. She reached across the car and gripped her daughter's hand as Mallory's tear-filled eyes found hers.

"I'm so sorry to complain about this," Mallory whispered. "It sounds so stupid, especially when I compare it to everything else."

"It's not stupid. You should be able to find love in every-thing Lucas does for you. He should support you in every single possible way."

Mallory's chin quivered again. "Maybe I ask for too much. I just feel so alone sometimes. And Lucas even goes out to see his friends all the time, and there I am, in that little apartment, wondering if we'll ever be able to get something bigger. Wondering if our lives will ever get past this bickering and resolve into something so special, the way yours and Dad's did."

There was this feeling of being trapped by time. Elsa remembered it — remembered feeling that she would never be old enough for so many things. She had always felt that if she could just age up five more years, or ten more years, or maybe fifteen, she would have the kind of peace and confidence that other people seemed to exhibit. The truth of it was much more complicated, and she knew that now.

"All you can do is demand what you need in this world and

draw your own boundaries," she told Mallory then. "Tell Lucas how you feel. Tell him everything, honey. You shouldn't be afraid to share your emotions."

"What if he can't be what I need him to be?"

Elsa gave the slightest of shrugs. "If he's not there for you, you know I will be— every single step of the way."

# Chapter Five

Elsa's mind rollicked with storms. There was tightness in her shoulders and an ache in her belly. Mallory, at only twenty-four-years-old, had begun to discover the secrets of real womanhood: that you had to be much, much stronger than everyone around you; that you had to be both the ship and the anchor; that you had to forgive, and then forgive again until you felt your bones crack with the weight of it all.

Her email inbox at the office blinked at her with an urgent number of emails. Nancy had already suggested that she hire a personal assistant — someone to type out email responses and keep track of her business meetings. Elsa had a stack of applications for this very position on her desk. Still, there was something about having someone so close to her business, knowing the ins and outs of her everyday life, that she resisted.

Elsa crossed her hands over her lap. Outside her office, Janine's voice greeted someone warmly, and Elsa's stomach dropped lower with something that unfortunately resembled resentment. How had Elsa, 'one of the sweetest people anyone had ever met,' turned into such a sour creature?

Janine herself appeared in her office seconds later with a stack of mail. Her skin glowed as she rushed toward Elsa's desk and placed the letters to the right of her keyboard. "Ooph! I have to run. I don't know why I did it to myself, but I arranged three back-to-back appointments this afternoon."

Just as Janine snaked out of the office and closed the door, Elsa found her voice enough to say, "Thanks for the mail."

She exhaled somberly and lifted the first letter, then the second. Most seemed to be bills for the Katama Lodge itself; others were information from doctors that practiced off the island, who wanted to request to transfer their patients to the Lodge for wellness retreats. These doctors remained in the dark ages, the ones who still liked a paper trail. Neal had been fond of these sorts of doctors. "I just don't like the new ways. It's so impersonal," he'd said frequently.

At the bottom of the stack, Elsa found a strange letter from Canterbury, attorney-at-law. Her thumb snuck beneath the fold and tore the paper straight across. In a flash, she had the thick letter out before her.

And in a moment, her entire body filled with dread.

*To Whom It May Concern,*

*We are the attorneys who represent Carlson Montague, a previous client of the now-deceased Aiden Steel. Carlson Montague has reason to believe that Aiden Steel mishandled an enormous amount of funds, in which he will be pressing charges against the entire Steel estate.*

Elsa's eyes grew. Her fingers let the letter fly loose, and it fluttered to the ground.

Press charges against the entire STEEL ESTATE.

That meant press charges against her own livelihood. It meant press charges against her, and her memory, and Aiden's memory. Everything he stood for.

It was an assault on everything she held dear to her heart. How could this be happening?

And above everything else, she didn't believe it was true. Aiden had been a remarkably kind-hearted man. He had assisted his clients, made enormous funds for them, assisted them on their journey to wealth and prosperity, and never complained a single day in his life. In return, his clients had often sent along beautiful Christmas gifts and very cheerful letters of thanks. This letter, in fact, was the first Elsa had ever heard with any kind of malice.

She kind of wanted to punch something.

Elsa retrieved the letter from the floor and reread it as though it might give her some fresh perspective. When it remained the same, she bolted for the door. Her eyes filled with bright spots as she wandered, helpless. She felt on the verge of a panic attack as her heart pounded in her chest, threatening to burst through her rib cage. She headed straight for Nancy's yoga studio but found that the door was closed tight as Nancy was in the midst of instructing a child's pose meditation. Elsa blinked out across the twelve women, all with their bodies tucked tight against their mats. "Inhale and slowly exhale." Nancy's words floated above and then shivered under the doorframe.

Elsa rushed down the hall then and headed for Janine's office. After all, wasn't the woman her stepsister, someone she was supposed to eventually rely on? But when she arrived at Janine's door, she heard a patient within; her voice was muffled as she described whatever current trauma she found herself in. "I feel so broken," the patient whimpered. "I just don't know what to do."

The sides of the letter crumpled in Elsa's hand. Her knees clacked together as she continued down the hallway. She wasn't sure where she was headed; she no longer felt minutes passing, nor her feet on the ground. She eventually burst out onto one of the porches that overlooked Katama Bay. This was where she fell to her knees as her head spun round and round in circles.

She was totally alone in this world. Everything had fallen upon her shoulders, and there was nothing she could do.

Suddenly, there was a hand on her back. There was a calming, soothing voice. There were eyes before her as a beautiful woman crouched down and whispered, "Elsa? Hey? Hon? Are you okay?"

Elsa dropped her teeth over her lower lip as she fell into Carmella's eyes. It was remarkable, really, how much Carmella looked like their mother, Tina, who had passed away when Elsa had been sixteen years old. Tina had been about Carmella's age at the time. Their eyes flickered with similar versions of loss and sorrow.

"Can you stand?" Carmella asked as she drew a strand of hair behind Elsa's ear.

Elsa swallowed the lump in her throat. "I don't know."

"Okay. We can just stay here for a minute, then. Nobody else is here. It's just us."

It had been so long since Carmella had spoken so kindly to Elsa before. Still, Elsa felt herself building a wall. She and Carmella had been through too much; it was akin to the story of the scorpion and the frog. How often had Carmella reared her ugly head and stung her?

Elsa's eyes hardened. In return, Carmella's did as well. Carmella shifted back and removed her hand from Elsa's shoulder.

"Have you eaten something today?" Carmella asked finally.

Elsa shrugged as she folded up the letter from the Canterbury lawyers. "I just wanted to get some fresh air."

Carmella's smirk was only slightly unkind. "Come on. Come to my office."

Elsa resisted at first. Slowly, Carmella lifted her back to her feet, and she draped her arm along Elsa's waist to ensure she remained standing. Elsa longed to compliment Carmella on her perfume. It was simmering sandalwood and jasmine. She imagined Carmella's acupuncture patients adored it for its personality and the calm it brought.

But she wasn't necessarily in the habit of complimenting Carmella. Neither of them had bothered much in the way of such niceties in, oh, thirty years.

"I'm really okay," Elsa forced herself to say, even as her voice quivered.

"I've known you my whole life, Elsa. You don't look okay. Not even in the slightest."

Elsa bristled again. They were at the end of a long hallway, headed straight for Carmella's office. But she yanked herself back hard so that Carmella jumped away from her and glared.

"Just let me help you," Carmella said.

Elsa swept the letter into her back pocket and lifted her chin. "It's really nothing."

"What is that paper? You're hiding it."

"I'm not hiding anything," Elsa returned.

"Is there something going on with the Lodge?" Carmella demanded. "Are we in some kind of trouble? Was Dad keeping something from us?"

Elsa's eyes widened with anger. "Are you kidding me? Dad would never do anything wrong. He would never leave us in a lurch."

Carmella flipped her hair behind her shoulder. "Whatever."

"What do you mean, whatever?"

"It's just that, even if Dad had done something wrong, you would probably do everything in your power to hide it from me."

"That's ridiculous," Elsa blurted.

"It's not. You were always his golden child. In your eyes, he could do no wrong. And even if he did do wrong, you always turned yourself away."

"This isn't about Dad!"

Carmella scoffed again. She crossed her arms over her chest as she continued to assess Elsa. "There's something really wrong about you. I've noticed it the past few weeks. Not that you'd let me get close enough to you to ask you about it until now. Apparently, I'm the only one available to pick you up off the ground."

"This is why I can't turn to you for anything," Elsa returned. "You just make me feel guilty for showing any weakness."

"No. I just hate that you won't ever admit what's wrong. You brush everything aside. Whatever that letter is — it's huge. And because of your pride, you won't let me know what it's about, even if I could help."

"Well, you can't help. So can we please just drop it already?"

"How do you know? Why are you always thinking that I can't help?"

Elsa remained silent. Carmella scoffed again.

"This is unbelievable," Carmella muttered. "You know what? Whatever, Elsa. Next time I find you in a heap on the floor, I'll just walk right past."

Carmella turned on her heel after that and made her way back toward her office; her heels clacked across the floor ominously. When her door slammed shut behind her, Elsa again collapsed and leaned heavily against the wall. She willed herself to keep her tears inside. She had to be strong enough for herself and, now, for Aiden's memory. She had to find a way to fight back.

# Chapter Six

The only answer Elsa had was to drive back to the very house she'd avoided over the previous year. She blew off everything that afternoon, including all meetings and emails, and sped all the way there. Tears stained her blouse; sweat pooled across the back of her neck. The sun felt entirely too close, and the world felt like it had shifted off its axis all because of this horrible man, Carlson Montague, who was trying to stain Aiden's reputation, and suing his estate after his death was enraging. And it was up to her to fight back and protect her family name—her husband's name.

Elsa had hired someone to maintain and fix up the property in her absence. A gardener came around once per week to tend to the bushes and the flowers; a maid frequently came to dust and did minor chores. As far as she knew, these were the only people who had gone in and out of the house since she'd closed it up the year prior. Admittedly, she had gone there once, with her father in tow, to retrieve some of her more nostalgic Christmas decorations, as she hadn't been able to understand a Christmas without them. Neal had been a stronghold for her;

he had stood by her side as she'd searched through the big old boxes and crates for the relevant items. When she had burst into tears at the sight of Aiden's old leather jacket, he had held her until she'd found a way to go on. "I don't know how I could have done this without you, Daddy," she'd told him only a few weeks before he joined Aiden in heaven.

Elsa's key fob for the garage door remained on her keychain. She hit the button, and just as it always had, the garage door yanked up from the ground to reveal the old garage with its second refrigerator, unused bicycles, and all of Aiden's tools. The place was already a minefield of memories, and she still hadn't found a way inside, where the real painful memories began.

The kitchen smelled of lemon cleaning supplies and nothing else. This was strange for a kitchen that had once flourished with Elsa's endless array of cooking concoctions. It had been pleasurable for her to make up new recipes for her husband and children. Even when her children had grown, she'd demanded that they meet at the dining room table once a week to swap stories from their separate lives. *"I want us to stay a close-knit family,"* she'd told Aiden. *"I know it's possible. We just have to be strict about it."* When Alexie had gone off to NYU, she'd come at least once a month — something that had pleased her, as she'd felt it proof of the strength of the backbone of their family.

Now, she hadn't seen Alexie all summer. Probably, she found it too difficult to return. The island hummed with endless memories. She couldn't blame her. The passing of their father was so hard on all the kids.

Elsa wandered down the hallway. All the bedroom doors had been closed, and she didn't dare open them. Each room would have been an assault on her senses. Already, she could practically hear the variety of voices that had once purred through the halls. Mallory, as a teenager, hollering to Alexie to stay out of her room. Cole blasting Nirvana from his bedroom. Their cat, who had also passed on, slinking through their legs and meowing. It had all happened. If she closed her eyes, she could pretend it was all still there.

Aiden had frequently worked from home. Elsa had never liked spending time in his office. It was his place of solitude, his place of privacy and where he took important phone calls with clients. Aiden had even been the one to decorate it. He had hung an old painting of a whaling boat on the far wall, and he'd lined the opposite wall with books his father had passed on to him when he had died. She placed her finger along the spines of these books and remembered how she'd marveled at the iconic collection:

*Shakespeare.*
*Moby Dick.*
*The Count of Monty Cristo.*
*The Unbearable Lightness of Being.*

Aiden had gotten around to quite a few of them. He always took these thick books to the beach while Elsa had immersed herself in her style and gossip magazines. *"That looks like so much fun,"* she'd often teased him sarcastically. *"You're so good at just kicking back and keeping things light."*

Elsa sat in the chair he'd so often sat in and blinked down at the glow of the antique wood of his desk. Probably, there was paperwork regarding this Carlson Montague fellow some-where. Aiden had been religiously organized and kept every-thing. Beneath the desk, there were a number of files filled with folders. She leafed through them and discovered a number of accounting papers from the previous twenty years. None of it seemed in any way relevant to any clients. Behind that box was another, but the paperwork was foreign to her, just a collection of numbers and pay rates and signatures. Her heart hammered with resentment toward her own failings. If only she under-stood more of what her husband had done. Sometimes, when he'd tried to explain something to her, she'd batted her eyelashes playfully and said, "I'm glad you understand these things because I certainly don't." Obviously, she would have been able to understand it if she'd applied herself; she wasn't dense. It was just that, with Aiden, she'd always felt like a teenager in love. She hadn't wanted to dwell on their everyday, humdrum careers. They had both agreed long ago to leave their work at work once finished for the day. When it was time for family time, she'd wanted magic.

Aiden had liked this about her. He'd said that it was so easy to forget about work around her. Their time together was always special.

Finally, Elsa did find a collection of paperwork that seemed relevant for his work with clients. Still, she couldn't focus enough to hunt for Carlson Montague's name. She even recognized a few of the signatures from people Aiden had known on the island, clients he had worked with for years. She bit down on her lower lip as her heart hammered. Nothing about this seemed logical. Mishandling of funds? What kind of proof did these people think they had?

Elsa knew she needed to speak to someone. She'd recently learned that Susan Sheridan, Wes Sheridan's eldest daughter, had opened a law office in Oak Bluffs. She rushed through her phone, on the hunt for the phone number. After three rings, a young woman answered.

"Good afternoon, this is the law office of Susan Sheridan. Amanda speaking. How can I help you?"

Elsa swallowed the lump in her throat. She had very little idea of what to say next. "Hello. My name is Elsa. Elsa Remington Steel." *Why had she said her entire name? Was she losing her mind?* "I was curious if I could speak with someone about a particularly strange situation I'm in."

Elsa did her best to describe small details of the letter, along with what she knew about her husband's work. "The complicated thing is, my husband died last year, and I'm terrified that these people not only want his money—my money—but that they also want to defame him."

"Of course, I understand, completely." Amanda paused on the other line for a long moment. "A difficult problem we have, unfortunately, is that my mother, Susan, has quite a packed schedule over the next few weeks. We've recently hired a new lawyer who's moved back to the island after years of working in Boston."

Elsa didn't care who she spoke to. She just needed a lifeline.

"His name is Bruce Holland," Amanda continued. "And he has a slot available as early as this next Tuesday. Are you available at four thirty?"

Elsa had zero comprehension of what day or time it even was at that moment. "Yes. That works," Elsa affirmed. "Thank you."

Amanda then asked for a number of details, including Elsa's phone number and email address. Elsa delivered everything with a solid voice; she was shocked that it didn't waver. When Amanda said, "Then we'll see you next week, Mrs. Steel," Elsa longed to ask the girl to remain on the phone a little bit longer. She didn't want to be alone. It was awful to be alone.

Elsa found herself in the darkening shadows of Aiden's office after that. She drew open several other desk drawers unconsciously, which was how she ultimately discovered the aged scotch, which, apparently, Aiden had saved for a rainy day. Elsa herself had never been particularly fond of scotch. When Aiden had poured himself something like that, she had always gone for white wine.

But always, when she'd kissed him, he had tasted of scotch.

And she wanted to taste that right now.

Elsa grabbed one of his tumbler glasses and poured herself

a finger of scotch. The aroma became a cloud over everything else. She lifted the glass toward the ceiling and muttered, "I won't let them do this to you, Aiden. I promise you that." She then took a sip and scrunched her nose. Memories flooded over her. Suddenly, all she wanted to do was drink and forget.

She'd never been that kind of drinker before. The thought of it frightened her, even as she poured herself another glass.

What the heck would happen next?

Would this Carlson Montague really drag her and her family through the mud without so much as even batting a lash? She didn't know if she would survive it.

How could she prove that this was some kind of mistake if she couldn't make heads or tails of the paperwork in her husband's office?

One scotch turned to three. The grandfather clock in the study had long since stopped its ticking; it was stuck at two thirty-three in the morning. The only way Elsa knew that time passed was because of the way the soft yellow light shifted to an orange hue. Her mind buzzed strangely and she could hear the whooshing of blood in her ears. A long time ago, Cole had discovered some of his father's whiskey in the upper cabinet in the kitchen; he and his teenage friends had drank maybe three or four glasses and passed out in front of the television. Their hangovers had been so colossal that Aiden and Elsa had agreed not to punish him too terribly. Cole had never been a big drinker after that. Proof, maybe, that you had to make your own mistakes in order to learn from them.

But Elsa wasn't fully sure of which mistakes had led her to this dark moment. She tried to play out all the events in her mind — from the moment she'd met Aiden as a teenager, to the moment Cole had been born (just about five months before their wedding), to the moment she had walked down the aisle to say her vows. She strained to remember every bad day, every marriage tiff, every time they'd said things they hadn't meant.

Still, only blurred, beautiful memories made their way through.

How grateful she was for all of it.

But now, it seemed like she'd lived out the best days of her life, and she was left with whatever the rest of this was— this mess that could potentially destroy her, her family, and their good name.

# Chapter Seven

The light snapped on overhead. Elsa's eyes popped open, then immediately closed, as the impact of the light created wave after wave of pain and fear through her forehead and then back through the base of her skull. There was a sound— a voice, but Elsa's head banged so heavily with a headache that she found it difficult to articulate what exactly she heard.

*Where was she?* The question demanded an answer, even as she realized she hadn't asked herself anything like this in her life. She had been the eternal responsible one, the one who'd demanded that others drink water before bed, and the one who always had her alarm clock set for the proper time, despite usually rising ahead of time and jumping in the shower without pause.

She was on a mattress. This much was clear so far — although the scratchy nature of the fabric beneath her arms and naked legs told her that the mattress had nothing over it, not even a sheet. She'd never slept on a bare mattress before, either. She had always cornered Cole about this in his younger days while attending college when she would visit him. "I just pass out sometimes," he'd told her somberly, his hand over the base of his neck. "I'll try to remember to be better." This had broken her heart still more, that he'd felt so embarrassed in front of his perfectionist mother.

"Look at me now, Cole," she grumbled now.

"Elsa? Can you hear me?"

Finally, the voice in the room yanked her from her reverie. Elsa turned her head the slightest bit in the direction of the voice as she whispered, "Can you turn the light off, so I can open my eyes?"

In a moment, the light snapped off again and cast everything in a somber gray light. Elsa slowly lifted her eyelids and blinked several times.

"Elsa? You're scaring me."

There was pressure off to the right of Elsa's body as the person sat. After another blink, Elsa recognized Nancy beside her. Her brow furrowed with worry, and her eyes were glossy, as though she had recently been crying. She placed a hand over Elsa's, there on the mattress, as understanding fell over her.

She wasn't on just any mattress. She was on the mattress she had once shared with Aiden, in the house they'd shared and raised their kids in. She hadn't slept in it since the night before Aiden had passed.

And oh, yes. She'd gotten hammered in Aiden's office because of the letter that was poised to ruin her life even more.

"What time is it?" Elsa finally asked.

"It's just past eleven."

Elsa's heart surged into her throat. She tried to yank herself up from the mattress, but the hangover dragged her back to the depths as her head throbbed with pain. "No. No, that's not right," she told no one in particular. "I don't understand."

"Shh." Nancy drew a line from Elsa's hand up toward her elbow. "I'm just glad I found you. I was so worried when you didn't come home last night. Janine told me to let it go, that you were an adult and could do what you wanted with your time. But I panicked when you didn't come into the Lodge this morning."

Elsa clenched her eyes once more, then shook her head ominously. Her soul felt black. "I can't even tell you how sorry I am. I totally lost my mind."

"Hey. You're allowed to lose your mind every once in a while." Nancy tried out a small laugh, but it fell flat. "Do you want to tell me what happened?"

Elsa really did want to tell someone about the letter, about the horror of realizing that so much was about to come crumbling down on her head. But her throat was parched, her thoughts had no gravity, and she thought she might hurl.

Finally, she whispered, "What about your classes today? I don't want you to miss your work."

Nancy waved a hand back and forth. "I must have told you that we hired that new yoga instructor— the young one. She's around twentysomething and can work nonstop, all day long, it seems like. I asked her to take over my classes for the morning and early afternoon. It's not a problem at all."

Elsa buzzed her lips. Resentment for herself, her situation, and everything rose to her throat.

"I have to say. This doesn't look very comfortable," Nancy commented as she scanned the mattress Elsa was lying on. Again she let out a slight laugh.

"I don't think I cared at some point. I just needed something soft to lie on," Elsa returned. "I feel pathetic."

Nancy reached for something on the bedside table and then lifted a little brown bag and a cup of to-go coffee into the air. "Look. I brought you those croissants from the Sunrise Cove and their coffee. I know you think it's the best on the island."

Elsa groaned. This act of love and allegiance made her feel

even worse. For weeks, she'd felt that Nancy wanted to abandon her for her "real" daughter; it was clear, now, that Elsa had been acting foolish, like a jealous teenager.

"Thank you," she moaned as she lifted up and pressed herself against the headboard. She took the first sip of coffee, and a few clear thoughts immediately sprang into her mind. "Gosh, I can't believe this. I can't believe I just didn't even go into work. What kind of person am I? I've never done that."

"Don't beat yourself up about it. It happens to the best of us." Nancy's voice warmed. She scooted the slightest bit onto the mattress so she could cross her perfect legs beneath her. "I want to ask you something. And I want you to answer as honestly as you can."

"Okay."

"Do you think you maybe weren't really ready to return to the Lodge?"

Elsa allowed her eyes to close again. She felt so much behind this question: earnest love, the kind that seemed straight from her father's heart. Nancy and Neal had been so close that they'd frequently finished one another's sentences. It was like Neal had fallen into her and used Nancy as a conduit to check in on Elsa.

"I don't know," Elsa said finally. "I wanted to be ready. You and Janine and Carmella seemed so excited about it. I tried to fall in line with anyone else and it felt good for a while. At the party, I told myself that I had to keep it together. That it was so clear the island needed us. But now..."

Nancy nodded earnestly.

For a moment, Elsa considered telling Nancy everything about the letter she had received regarding her and Aiden's estate. But it seemed too difficult to explain.

It was better to keep this private for now. She didn't want anyone, not even Nancy, to think a single ill thought about

Aiden. In Elsa's eyes, Aiden was the perfect man. Nobody could take that away or tarnish his good name.

"Why don't you take some time off?" Nancy asked as she tilted her head. "You deserve it."

"No way," Elsa told her. "I had one off day. It won't happen again. I can promise you that."

Nancy pressed her lips together as though she wanted to say something more but willed herself to keep it in. She sighed, then said, "You're so much like Neal. So stubborn and always putting everyone else above yourself."

Elsa blinked quickly to hold her tears in. "I just miss him so much."

"I know. Me too, honey."

Nancy stepped out of the room for a moment to grab Elsa a glass of water. Elsa took further stock of herself. She had apparently removed her suit pants and suit jacket, so she just lay there in a tank top and a pair of underwear. Apparently, she'd dragged one of Cole's old blankets with his high school logo smattered all over it out of the closet, but she had kicked it to the side in the middle of the night.

By the time Nancy returned to the bedroom, Elsa had yanked on her pants and suit jacket once more. She thanked Nancy for the glass of water and drank the entire thing in a hurry. She then stepped into the en suite bathroom, where she found a grisly version of herself with stringy hair and pit stains and big bags under her eyes. This wasn't the Elsa Remington Steel she had built over the years. This was a sad, depressed widow.

"You should get back to work," Elsa hollered through the crack in the door. "I don't want to keep you."

Nancy grumbled. "Are you sure you don't need me? I'm here for you if you want that."

"Don't be silly. You know that I can handle anything." Elsa feigned her brightest smile, even as her insides screamed.

"Right, of course. Just like Neal." Nancy's smile fell the slightest bit as she gathered her purse over her shoulder. "I'll see you at home, then, right? You aren't moving back here?"

"No." Elsa shook her head violently. "I just, I don't know. I can't explain it. But thank you for finding me. I feel like I had some kind of, erm, mental break. But it's over now. I promise."

Nancy paused at the doorway and lifted her eyes to Elsa's. "You know, you don't have to be so strong all the time. We tell the women at the Lodge that, but, well, it's especially true for us, too."

Elsa squared her shoulders and prepared to respond with something bright and cheery. But before she could, Nancy disappeared into the darkness of the hallway. There was the *rap-rap-rap* of her shoes across the foyer, and then a moment later, she was gone.

This left Elsa in the reality of the truth: that no, she couldn't handle this by herself. But damn if she wasn't going to try.

# Chapter Eight

The yearly Round-the-Island sailing race was held every year in Edgartown Harbor. In previous years, Elsa had been very much involved in planning the extravagant party, as Aiden had been a prominent part of Martha's Vineyard sailing community. Aiden won the race frequently, and their house had a number of his trophies to prove it. The previous year, Elsa had avoided the festivities like the plague. She hadn't wanted to see the soulful, pitying eyes of the other sailors' wives, the ones she'd known for decades, as their own husbands embarked over the ocean waves. She hadn't wanted to acknowledge the depth of her sadness in the midst of the world Aiden had loved so dearly.

This year was different, though. Cole had announced months before that he planned to follow in his father's footsteps and race around the island with the others. His father had taught him everything there was to know about sailing; in fact, they'd gone out on their first expedition when Cole had been only seven years old. By that time, Cole had already spent a number of hours per night perfecting his sailing knots. He had dressed as a pirate for Halloween three years in a row. *"That boy is just like you,"* Elsa had teased Aiden. *"And God help us all."*

Elsa appeared at the docks as the first of the Edgartown race party began. A tent had been set up, and beneath it, a live band had begun to perform classic rock hits — stuff from Journey and the Eagles and Tom Petty, songs that Aiden had blared out in that wretched voice of his. Elsa informed herself that crying on this day wasn't an option. She wanted to have a good time. She wanted to be the other Elsa, the one she'd always been years before when cancer had just been something that happened to other people's husbands. What a fool she'd been.

Olivia Henson, a teacher at the nearby high school, brushed past her with a glass of wine, then turned her head brightly to say hello. "Elsa! You look amazing."

"Olivia, hello." Elsa hadn't seen much of Olivia since her youngest, Alexie, had graduated from high school. All of her children had adored Ms. Hesson; she had brought countless books to life for them and forced them to dig into their creativity, something far different than their typical science or math classes. "How are you doing?"

"Oh, I'm just fine. A bit stressed I guess," Olivia admitted.

"That's right! I read about it in the paper. The Hesson House just opened, didn't it?"

Olivia grimaced. "You're such a wonder for working in hospitality for so long. Honestly, I am so proud of that little boutique hotel. The last few months almost killed us trying to make sure everything was up to par and ready to go."

"But nothing is ever ready when it comes to tourists," Elsa said with a knowing laugh.

"I figured you'd get it," Olivia said.

"All too well."

"Maybe I could pick your brain sometime. You've done so remarkably for years at the Katama Lodge," Olivia said.

"Sure. Yeah. Let's find the time," Elsa said, even as her insides screamed just how little she wanted to help anyone with anything. It wasn't that she didn't care for Olivia or have the know-how to assist. She just felt so stretched thin; she felt she couldn't offer anything at all to anyone beyond her own daughter.

Speaking of which, where was Mallory? They'd agreed to meet at the party around this time.

"Anyway, I have to find my boyfriend, Anthony," Olivia told her as she peered through the crowd. "He's massive, so you'd think it wouldn't be this difficult to pick him out of the crowd. Maybe I'm going blind in my old age."

"We're not so old yet!" Elsa tried yet again to laugh, but it came out sour.

In truth, she felt about a million years old.

Elsa continued to weave through the crowd. She paused at a natural wine stall for a glass of orange wine, locally made from a Massachusetts winery; while there, she spotted Mallory, deep in the crowd. She wore a light yellow dress, which fluttered around her thighs. She had hired a babysitter for the afternoon. Elsa realized just how much she had missed her daughter and grandson since the last time she saw them at Neal's house. It had only been a few days, but somehow, she looked lighter, freer, like a young woman on top of the world, rather than a woman with a million responsibilities and a bickering fiancé, to boot.

Elsa waved a hand and caught Mallory's attention. Mallory's smile was electric and contagious. She rushed toward her mother and wrapped her arms around her. Elsa was reminded of the long-ago days when Mallory, Cole, and Alexie had greeted their parents in just this way. Elsa and Aiden had been their superheroes— their world. The switch of that from superhero to just another parent had been a difficult thing to grasp. Elsa and Aiden had teased one another about it frequently. "Well, I guess the magic's over. We had a good run."

"You look beautiful, Mom," Mallory commented as she gestured for the bartender to pour an additional glass of wine. "Where did you get that dress?"

"This? Oh. I dragged it out of the back of my closet." Elsa glanced down at the long black summer dress, with its slight cleavage and fluttering sleeves.

"What else do you have back there?" Mallory teased.

"I know, I know. I haven't dressed my best the past year," Elsa returned.

Mallory's smile faltered immediately. "I didn't mean that at all. Besides, if we're bringing past history into the mix, I haven't exactly spent a lot of time out of my sweatpants this past year."

Elsa lifted her wineglass for Mallory to clink hers against it. "Well then. Cheers to us, finally out of sweatpants."

Mallory laughed as the light returned to her eyes. "Now, that's something to celebrate."

Elsa and Mallory walked toward the starting line, where they spotted Cole toward the far end of the harbor, preparing his sailboat. The wind rushed through his dark hair and swept the strands back as he concentrated on the ropes, on his balance, and for a moment, he looked remarkably like his father some twenty-five years before — an earnest and confident young man, a man who could fully handle himself, a man who could operate an entire sailboat alone and probably place in the top three of the race, at least.

"There's Tommy Gasbarro," Mallory muttered as she nodded toward the docks, where the previous year's winner sauntered toward his own boat.

Tommy Gasbarro was a second-generation Italian sailor and the ex-stepson of Stan Ellis, the man who had been driving the boat that had crashed the night Anna Sheridan had died.

Tommy had won the race the previous year and then almost immediately scooped up Lola Sheridan, the third of the Sheridan sisters. They'd fallen in love and moved in together in a little cabin in the woods, the same one where Chuck Frampton had once resided—prior to his arrest for robbing a number of island businesses.

"He's so handsome, isn't he?" Mallory said with a smile.

"Your father always liked him," Elsa said. "Some of the other sailors weren't as kind. Tommy always kept to himself."

"Elsa! Mallory!"

Elsa whipped around to catch sight of Nancy as she swept through the crowd with a glass of wine. Janine hustled up behind her. Nancy and Janine were so close in age—sixteen years apart—that now, their faces reflected one another like mirror images. They could have passed as sisters.

Despite her occasional resentment for Nancy and Janine's budding relationship, Elsa's lips tugged into a smile. Nancy wrapped an arm around her shoulders and held her close. "There he is! That handsome Cole. He looks like a real man, doesn't he?"

"He sure does," Elsa breathed.

"Wow." Janine sidled in on the other side of Mallory and greeted them all warmly. "Look at all those sailboats. It's unreal. Oh, and look! There's Henry!"

Elsa peered out across the sailboats to find Henry, Janine's friend that she suspected would turn into a budding relationship with time. Elsa didn't feel close enough to Janine to press her for details; besides, she'd only just gotten out of her marriage about two months before. But the way Janine lifted her hand to wave at the handsome documentarian told Elsa they were extremely close. You could practically feel Janine's heart rising in her chest with excitement.

"He hasn't raced since his twenties," she explained.

"He's really taken island life back, hasn't he?" Nancy stated as she turned back to the water.

The sailboats lined up then. There was the blast of the starting gun, and then, full-blown white sails filled like balloons. Elsa forgot herself and reached for her daughter's hand, which she squeezed hard as Cole struck out into the wild breeze and soon disappeared on the far side of the Edgartown lighthouse.

"There he goes," Elsa breathed, to no one in particular.

Mallory flashed Elsa a wide grin. Her eyes were heavy with tears. "I remember coming here as a little girl and standing right here as Dad raced. I always begged for him to take me around the island for the race."

Elsa laughed. "Yes, but when it came time for him to teach you how, you always had something better to do, remember?"

"I was such a horrible teenager."

"That's not true at all. You were just typical. You liked your friends and your boyfriends. Your dad got it."

"Not sure I deserved how understanding he was," Mallory returned.

"Maybe none of us did," Elsa finished.

Nancy, Janine, Mallory, and Elsa gathered around a tall table as the boats circled the island. Another band walked onto the stage as several islanders passed them by and said hello. Elsa willed her smile to grow brighter; she prayed that her laughter sounded genuine and not fake. Still, she felt everyone's pity and everyone's words—that they only wished both Aiden and Neal could be there with them, like the old times—and it really didn't help at all.

Nancy and Janine fell into another walk down memory lane. This left Mallory and Elsa to stir in their own anxieties about the current situation. Elsa's eyes searched the horizon line for some sign of Cole; all the while, she tried to drum up some way to ask Mallory about her situation with Lucas. She had avoided the topic since she'd first brought it up, but Elsa didn't want to have that sort of relationship with her daughter. She didn't want anything brushed under the rug.

She was there for her till the end. She had to be. There was no one else around.

"Mal, you'd tell me if anything was wrong, wouldn't you?" Elsa finally asked as she swirled the wine in her glass.

Mallory grimaced and turned her eyes toward the ground.

"I guess that's a no?" Elsa asked softly.

"I just don't want to think about it."

"You know, you can stay with Nancy and me if you want," Elsa breathed. "We're always here for you, no matter what."

Mallory's eyes flickered with sunlight. "I don't know. I don't want to make him even angrier."

"Women have been there for one another since the dawn of time, especially when their partners fail them," Elsa returned.

Mallory's chin quivered. "I don't want Zachery to fail anyone when he's older."

Elsa's laugh was soft, tentative. "Unfortunately, all you can do is show him how to love and love well. Maybe Lucas can't offer him those teachings, but you can. You love better than anyone. Besides, you both have plenty of time to worry about that. He's only a baby."

"Hey, girls! Do you want another glass of wine?" Nancy's voice carried through their conversation and obliterated it. Hurriedly, Mallory swiped a hand beneath her eye to catch her tear.

"Of course," Mallory said brightly. "Thank you, Nancy."

With Nancy gone, Janine turned toward them and said, "Henry was up in arms about Cole the other night. He said there were two sailors he was really nervous about on the water. Cole Steel and Tommy Gasbarro. He said he didn't have a chance."

Mallory's laughter rang out beautifully, like a song. "My

brother learned everything from our dad. He's racing for him out there, now."

When the first sails flickered up over the horizon line, Elsa gripped Mallory's hand and muttered, "I really think that might be him. Is it? Gosh, I can't—"

"It's him!" Mallory cried as Cole's sailboat swept toward the finish line. Cole Steel himself leaned forward as the wind swept through his hair; his nose was lifted toward the starkly blue sky above, and his eyes spoke of determination. It was clear, beyond a shadow of a doubt, that Cole Steel had come to the competition to win. He wouldn't have allowed it any other way.

Elsa and Mallory shrieked as his sailboat surged forth; there was the sound of an alarm, then the wailing cries of hundreds of partygoers and revelers. Elsa and Mallory wrapped their arms around one another and hollered as they hugged. They then turned toward Janine and Nancy for more hugs and cries and calls of, "I knew he had it in him!" and, "He did this for Aiden! It's all for Aiden!"

Elsa hadn't felt so overzealous in years. She leaped toward the docks, where one of the festival organizers stepped toward Cole and swept out a hand to shake his. "Congratulations, son!" the man cried as another sailboat—the second-place finisher, Tommy Gasbarro—surged toward the docks.

Tommy tied up his boat, his brow was furrowed, but his eyes were alight. "Cole Steel, dammit, I nearly had you out there by the cliffs. I thought to myself — that boy is fresh meat. But no, here you are, in first place. You should be proud." The older man leaped from the boat and smacked Cole across the back as Cole beamed at him.

You could see it in everything Cole did: he was shocked that he'd beaten such a confident sailor. Tommy Gasbarro had sailed all over the world, frequently alone. But Cole, who had hardly stepped foot off the island of Martha's Vineyard, had pulled off a win.

As Tommy spoke to the festival organizer, Cole's gaze found his mother's. His long legs snaked him down the dock as his smile grew wider. It seemed impossible that this twenty-six-year-old man had once been the tiniest of babies, two weeks early with ten tiny fingers and toes.

"Mom!" He flung his arms around her as Elsa burst into tears.

"I'm so proud of you! Your father would be so proud of you!" she cried as she pushed his hair out of his face.

How strange it was to hug this much taller man. His muscles still pulsed from the adrenaline of the race. When he fell back, his grin faltered the slightest bit. Under his breath, he said, "I just wish he could have been here, racing beside me."

"I know, honey. Me too." Elsa cleared her throat, then added, "Maybe you would have beaten him, too. He wouldn't have known what to do about that."

Cole cackled. "I would have never let him hear the end of it. That's for sure."

# Chapter Nine

The award ceremony was held immediately after the race, beneath a large white tent, the top of which reflected the severity of the July sun. In the shadowy comfort beneath, Elsa, Janine, Nancy, and Mallory huddled close and watched as the announcer cleared his throat into the microphone, then began in that smooth, rich voice of his — the likes of which was heard at most Martha's Vineyard festivals and events over the summer months. He provided the backdrop of so much.

"Good afternoon, ladies and gentlemen, and welcome to another marvelously successful Round-the-Island sailing race, which we hold every year here in the beautiful town of Edgartown. As many of you know, the sailing community here on Martha's Vineyard is quite tight-knit. Everyone knows everyone, and we get mighty sick of one another sometimes—"

At this, the crowd chuckled good-naturedly as the announcer's eyes flashed across the sea of people.

"But in the end, we're all there for one another. We're one another's neighbors, friends, and family. We're there when the wind is fresh for sailing, and we're there when the storms roll in from the horizon and tear our sails apart. Many of you know what it's like when you're out there on the open seas, terrified about what will happen next, yet trusting your gut and your adrenaline to get you home."

Elsa had been out on the water with Aiden only once when a storm had thrust itself upon them. She had gone into overdrive as Aiden had instructed her on what to do next. With each step she'd taken, each rope she'd yanked, she'd pictured her three babies at home waiting for them, so they had to return. There was no option otherwise.

"This brings me to my next point," the announcer continued. "Last year, around this time, we lost one of our own. He was a true pillar of the sailing community and a man that many of us loved like a brother or like a father or like a son. His name was Aiden Steel, and our love for him and his leadership in this community will never die.

"For this reason, I am pleasantly pleased to announce this year's winner of the Round-the-Island race," the announcer continued. "Cole Steel! Come on up here, you son of a gun."

Cole leaped up onto the stage. His smile was so electric; there were flashes of a much younger version of himself simmering around behind those eyes. He accepted the award, a golden-colored sailboat with the year listed beneath the boat, on a mahogany piece of wood. He then lifted the award into the air as the crowd cried out with excitement. All the while, Elsa and Mallory held hands while yelling and screaming his name. "WE LOVE YOU, COLE!"

The announcer passed the microphone to Cole. Cole had always been on the shyer side and he'd never been one for big gestures or grand speeches. But when he took the microphone in hand, there was a severity to his eyes; it was clear that he had something to say.

"Good afternoon, everyone, and thank you. Thank you, from the bottom of my heart," Cole said.

"He sounds so good," Mallory breathed to Elsa.

"I just want to take a moment to say some words about my dad," Cole continued as his voice wavered just the slightest bit. "My father was the strongest and most passionate man I've ever met. Throughout my childhood, I begged him to take me out on the water. In the beginning, he told me, 'Okay, you can come. But you have to promise that you won't complain. Not even when you're tired, or you're too hot, or you're too cold. Out there, you're at the mercy of the ocean and the waves and the elements. You are no longer tied to your physical needs.'

"I always took what he said to heart, and over time, I manned up and proved myself to him as a sailor. When he got sick, though, I just couldn't rationalize it. It seemed crazy to me that this man who had been able to override every single conceivable 'physical need' had to succumb to, well, his physical body and its failings. It was monstrous to me, but of course, it was much worse for him. For a long time, I could see him battling his mind, especially when he could no longer do all the things he wanted to do — like even walk on the beach with my mother, or go horseback riding with my sister, or bear wrestle my younger brother."

Cole paused and dropped his eyes toward his award, which he lifted a bit higher. Elsa prayed he wouldn't burst into tears; she could practically feel it coming through his words, like a storm. His face was marred with so many emotions that sprang tears in Elsa's eyes.

"I would trade this trophy in a flash if I knew I could spend one more day with my dad," Cole said finally. "But I also have to admit, I feel him closer, here at this festival, than I have in the past year since he died. This one is for you, Dad! Thank you for all of your support. And thank you for loving my father as much as you did. I know it meant the world to him."

In the wake of Cole's speech, the partygoers under the tent burst into applause; they wolf-whistled and hollered Cole's name. Cole ducked back down into the crowd and swept toward his little group of friends, some of the guys he'd gone to high school with, along with a girl Elsa had been curious about, as she'd suspected there was something romantic between them. Her eyes caught Cole's just then, and she blew him a kiss as he winked back at her. Her heart swelled with love for her son. She was so proud of him.

Nancy swept her lips toward Elsa's ear as she called, "He really is a remarkable young man."

Elsa nodded. "He's really something, isn't he?"

After the second and third place awards were given out, a DJ bolted over to the speaker system and began to play a wild collection of hits from the previous twenty years. The beat pumped through the crowd as revelers turned toward one another and fell into easy conversation. The line for drinks soon grew monstrously long; it snaked around the sides of the tent and then barreled out toward the docks.

"I can't believe that speech," Janine said to the three of them as she sipped up the last of her wine. "I really want him to meet my girls. I think Maggie and Alyssa and Cole would get along so well. Has Alexie looked up Maggie or Alyssa in the city yet?"

Elsa realized she'd again forgotten to remind her youngest to look up her new, super-rich, Manhattan socialite "cousins." Her stomach panged with guilt.

"I think she's so busy these days," Elsa lied. "She has two jobs, and she's taking a few classes over the summer."

"These kids. I don't know how they balance so much at once," Janine returned.

A friend of Mallory's had drawn her off to the side; the two of them purred with gossip. Elsa felt suddenly on edge and strange. She could practically feel Janine and Nancy's attempts to zero in on her and bring her into their conversation. Grateful for an out, she spotted Cole toward the back of the drink line, alone.

As she approached him, several partygoers stepped up to shake his hand and congratulate him. Cole seemed visibly drained; his smile no longer had its previous luster. When another man walked off, post-handshake, Elsa appeared behind him, and Cole's shoulders slumped forward with relief.

"I'm getting so tired," he said.

"I bet." Elsa stepped into the line to join him and swept her hand down his back. "I'm so proud of you, honey. I know your father is up there right now smiling down on you."

Cole flashed her a knowing smile before the exhaustion took over again, "Feels like I'll probably be here all night."

"You are the guest of honor, after all."

"Yeah." Cole's eyes grew shadowed. "I keep wanting to pinch myself. None of the past year feels real."

Elsa nodded. "I feel the same way."

The line grew longer. Elsa turned to watch as a number of broad-shouldered sailors, many of whom she recognized from the sailing club, shifted their weight and fell into conversation. Their eyes were glazed over from the alcohol; they didn't glance up, which Elsa was grateful for. She didn't want any more small talk about her husband. She didn't want to say, "Thank you, we miss him, too," all over again. It was exhausting.

But after a moment, her ears found a language that seemed completely foreign to her — as though they spoke about someone completely different.

"Can you believe we're supposed to be championing that fraud?"

"I know. We all know what he did."

"Blah blah — the sailing world's greatest loss! Give me a break."

Careful not to make any quick movements, Elsa turned her eyes toward the source of the conversation. Two men around Aiden's age stood with their brows furrowed. One was dark blond; the other had salt-and-pepper hair. Both were dressed all in white and had the general "air" of being incredibly wealthy, traditional sailing types. Elsa didn't recognize them at all.

"I mean, I told you what he did to me, didn't I?" the man with salt-and-pepper hair said.

"Of course," the other replied. "It's ridiculous. He was supposed to be God's gift to stockbroking, and now you have to deal with the aftermath."

The darker-haired man shook his head as his face grew shadowed with disdain. "Aiden Steel was no hero. He was a con artist. That's for sure."

At this, Cole bristled. He thrust himself around and glared at the two older men as he said, "Excuse me. What did you say about my father?"

Elsa's throat grew tight with fear. Everything about Cole's body seemed ready for attack.

"Oh, great. We have his second-in-command right here," the salt-and-pepper-hair man scoffed. He gave Cole a horrible grin. "What are you going to do, son? You want to stand up for your daddy's honor?"

Cole's right hand formed a fist. Elsa reached for his bicep and squeezed hard. Everything within her willed him not to do this, not here. Not ever. She hadn't raised a violent son.

"Just don't know why you think you can come here and spread lies about my father," Cole spat.

"That's right. We're spreading lies," the man said sarcastically as his eyes flashed.

"We get off on that kind of thing," the other returned. "Makes total sense, doesn't it?"

"Totally," the first said.

"Cole. Calm down," Elsa breathed.

"Listen to your mother, Cole," the first man said in a sarcastic tone.

Elsa's nostrils flared. She wanted to sock the man herself but held her ground. Still, she couldn't do anything about it. She yanked Cole back the slightest bit as his cheeks turned red as tomatoes.

"What the hell is all that about?" Cole demanded. His voice was hoarse with panic. "What the hell are they talking about? Con artist?"

Elsa shook her head. "Who knows, but we know it's not true. Your father didn't do anything wrong. He's an upstanding citizen and would never do anything shady."

At this, Cole's eyebrows lowered all the more. He yanked his arm out from her grip and said, "You know something."

Elsa bit hard on her lower lip. "I don't. I only know that people are trying to defame your father's name. And I'm in the middle of dealing with it."

"How can this be happening? What do you mean?" Cole demanded as spittle flew.

"I've hired a lawyer," Elsa returned. "But I don't want to talk about it here. Tonight is for celebrating. It's for honoring your father. It's not for stupid drunken fights with sailors who don't have a clue about what they're talking about. Okay? Do you hear me?"

Cole's brow remained furrowed, and his rage made his body shake. Elsa remained next to her son for the remainder of the line, all the way to the front, where she ordered a double vodka from the bartender, then ensured that her son joined his friends once again, rather than went after the sailors. When she returned to Mallory, Janine, and Nancy, Nancy commented that she looked "deathly pale."

"I think I need to head home soon," Elsa murmured as her stomach twisted into knots. "These wild parties are a part of my past, now."

In truth, she just couldn't stand there, knowing that these men were out there, defaming her husband.

She needed to focus; she needed to seek the truth and shut down this nonsense once and for all. And every raucous laugh, every wild cry through the crowd, made her feel increasingly alone.

# Chapter Ten

Elsa returned to the old house for a full ten minutes to retrieve the paperwork she had discovered in Aiden's office, just in case any of it was relevant for this new lawyer, Bruce Holland. She then shot out into the early afternoon sunlight and shoved the large box of papers into the back seat. Going into the house had felt almost an assault on her emotions, especially with her mind fresh with old memories. As she rushed back down the driveway and out onto the main road, she felt she moved overly fast, as though she ran from a previous version of herself, of her life.

She drove in a kind of a blur, all the way to Oak Bluffs. Once there, she realized she was a full hour early for her appointment with Bruce Holland. Annoyed at herself and her own anxious mind, she forced herself on a walk through the smoldering July heat. She paused for a moment at the historic Flying Horses Carousel, which had been placed in Oak Bluffs all the way back in 1884. Children in various stages of sugar-overdose wrapped their legs on either side of each beautiful steed and hollered at their parents as the carousel drew them round and round in circles.

If only Elsa could find such pleasure in life again. And in fact, she remembered long-ago days when her own father had brought her to this very carousel. The first few times, she had been too panicked to ride alone, and he had stood alongside her with his steady hand on her back. She had been mesmerized by the flashing lights and the bright music. It was like being transported to another world. It had been magic.

Things weren't like magic any longer. Not at forty-five. Not after so much death, sorrow and pain.

Elsa wandered along the waterline until she reached the Sunrise Cove Inn, which she hadn't seen much of since they had completely redone it the previous summer. The place had a fresh paint job; flowers bloomed from every conceivable location; even the trees outside of it looked fuller and more vibrant. It looked as it had in Elsa's memory, back in the days before Anna Sheridan's death.

Elsa stepped up to the bistro window, where a teenage boy sold her a cup of coffee and a freshly-baked croissant. He was boisterous and eager and thanked her for her service. "We're almost out of croissants for the day," he said. "Good thing you made it."

Elsa nibbled on the croissant and sipped her coffee on a bench just outside of Susan Sheridan's law office. Several tourists walked past, some with ice cream that dribbled across their cheeks. That was the thing about vacation, something Elsa craved: nothing mattered — not the ice cream on your face or the time of day or how loud you laughed. Everything was ultimate freedom.

Amanda Harris, Susan Sheridan's daughter, greeted Elsa in the foyer. She was the spitting image of her mother. "Hello, Mrs. Steel. How are you today?"

"Just fine, thank you," Elsa lied. She had grown accustomed to that lie over the previous year. "Sorry. I'm a bit early."

"Don't worry. Bruce is in his office. I'll see if he can take you already."

Elsa hovered near the front desk with her big box of paperwork. There was the muffled sound of voices as Amanda explained that his appointment was early. Then the door pushed open to reveal a broad-shouldered man of approximately six feet, four inches. He wore a nicely-cut suit — nothing too flashy and his seafoam green eyes found Elsa's immediately.

There was a comfort behind those eyes.

It was as though he, as a lawyer, working for people in the depths of despair, had learned how to generate this feeling of calm.

"Hello, Mrs. Steel," he greeted as he joined her in the foyer. "Let me take that box from you. It looks pretty heavy."

"Thank you." Elsa watched, amazed, as he lifted the thing from her arms as though it weighed nothing at all.

He held the box with his left hand as he reached out with his right to shake hers. "Welcome to the Sheridan Law Offices. Would you step into my office?"

Elsa followed him without a word and soon collapsed in the chair across from the main one as he closed the door behind them. His cologne was ever-present in the air over the desk — a cedar, sandalwood, and grapefruit combination that made Elsa feel incredibly alert. He wore a beard, which Elsa liked on him, and it was trim and fresh-looking, not like a hipster's or a lumberjack's.

"Amanda has brought me up to speed about what you told her on the phone," Bruce began as he folded his hands over the desk. "But I want to hear everything with your own words if it isn't too much trouble to go over it again. I don't want to miss any details."

Elsa pressed her lips together. In truth, she hadn't explained much of anything to anyone as of yet, and she found it difficult to uncover the narrative that the story required.

"My husband died a little over a year ago. He was a remarkable man. He worked as a stockbroker throughout essentially our entire marriage, and we were quite comfortable with his career alongside mine..."

"Which is?"

"I work as the public relations manager for the Katama Lodge and Wellness Spa." Elsa was surprised at the jolt of pride she felt as she said her title, despite the fact that she'd hardly managed to make it into the office the previous week.

"Ah yes. Neal Remington's place." Bruce tapped the tip of his pen against the desk.

"You're familiar with it?"

"Sure. I grew up on the island. Everyone knew Neal, even over here in Oak Bluffs. My father was friends with him before his own passing. I was sad to hear."

Elsa nodded somberly. "It was a real surprise for all of us. He'd had a few health problems, but nothing serious, so it was shocking, to say the least."

"He deserved a whole lot more time with his loved ones," Bruce said.

A lump formed in Elsa's throat and threatened to yank her into the depths of sorrow. Somehow, she kept her chin held high.

"I received this letter last week —" Elsa placed the letter on the desk and watched as Bruce read it. Slowly, his brow furrowed.

"I see." Bruce yanked out a notepad and began to scribble out notes for himself, none of which Elsa could possibly read — probably not even close-up.

"I also heard a few sailors at the Round-the-Island race discussing it," Elsa continued. "It seems like there are a number of people looking to defame my husband and take a huge amount of funds from his estate."

Bruce lifted his eyes toward hers. "I can't even imagine what you must be going through."

Elsa hadn't expected such empathy. The lump in her throat grew even bigger. "Yes, it's been hard, to say the least."

Bruce placed his pen down for a moment as his eyes held hers.

"I promise you that I will do everything in my power to get to the bottom of this and find some resolution. You have my word."

Elsa exhaled slowly. Her shoulders threatened to shake. "I just hate that his good name is already being dragged through the mud. He doesn't deserve this. He was always such a good and honest man."

Bruce set his jaw. After a moment, he said, "I understand. If someone had dragged my wife's name through the mud after her death, I would have lost my mind. All we have are our memories. And they're not only attempting to rob you of those; they're also trying to take your money. It's horrendous and an act of evil in my books."

Tears sprung to Elsa's eyes. How readily had this man brought the truth of his own life to the surface? Yet Elsa would have never known just by looking at him that he, too, had gone through some of the worst pain Elsa had ever experienced.

"I'm so sorry to hear that you lost your wife," she said softly.

Bruce nodded. "Thank you for saying that. It's part of the reason I came back to the Vineyard. I wanted a fresh start in a familiar place."

"Has it been welcoming, being back?" She asked, shifting in her seat.

Bruce considered this. "I'm still adjusting. I took the past year and a half off working in law to focus on myself, trying to heal. I'm sure you know that it can be difficult to maintain health when things get especially rough. That's one way of putting it, at least."

Elsa had the funniest urge to tell Bruce about her horrible scotch-fueled bender the previous week. Luckily, she held herself back and just said, "Yes. It's funny that amid so much sadness and pain, you have to remind yourself that you have a body that needs to be fed and maintained to keep yourself well."

"It's such a roller coaster," Bruce agreed.

Bruce returned his gaze to the letter before him and continued to jot notes off to the side. Elsa crossed and uncrossed her legs as panic eased out of her. She hadn't expected to feel so calm with her lawyer; she hadn't expected to find such empathy echoed back in his eyes.

"I guess I have my work cut out for me," Bruce said as he tapped the top of the stack of paperwork. "Lots to go over."

"Aiden was always very thorough. I just can't make heads or tails of anything in there," Elsa admitted.

"Don't worry. I'm a very lame superhero. I'm all paperwork and forms and legal jargon. It wouldn't make for a very good movie, but —"

"On the contrary, I think this is exactly the kind of super-hero the world needs." A warm smile stretched across Elsa's lips.

Elsa told Bruce to call her if he required anything at all. She even heard herself offer up Aiden's office if he wanted to search for more documents. As their conversation wound down, her legs turned to lead. She didn't want to leave that office. She'd found her knight in shining armor; she didn't want to return to the trenches of her own life just yet.

"I guess I'll see you very soon," Bruce said as he led her toward the door and shook her hand again. This time, Elsa fell into the flood of warmth, which beamed out from his hand.

It was difficult for her when they parted.

It was difficult for her to sit in the front seat of her car and stare straight ahead and visualize the next empty hours of her day.

It wasn't that she craved him in any way beyond the safety he offered.

Or maybe — just maybe he had reminded her, for the first time in over a year, that she wasn't dead yet. She hadn't fully realized that before; that for the majority of her time since Aiden had been lowered into his grave, she had considered herself more or less a corpse.

Bruce Holland was handsome, articulate, empathetic, and intelligent. He was on the case to save her husband's good name. It was a thrill to know him — a bright light in the darkness. And beyond anything, Elsa was just grateful he existed. That had to be enough.

# Chapter Eleven

As Elsa drove back to the house she shared with Nancy and Janine; her phone began to ring. She snapped a finger located just above the rearview, which allowed her speakerphone to come through the speakers of the car. Her phone remained latched away in her purse, and she answered with an air of professionalism, just in case it was a work call or something associated with Aiden's case.

"This is Elsa Steel speaking."

There was a strange croak on the other end of the line, then a sob echoed through. Elsa would have recognized the sound anywhere.

"Mallory? Honey? Are you okay?"

"Mom..." Mallory's voice wavered. Elsa could picture her daughter's face: scrunched tight marred with sadness, her eyes closed as she willed herself to stop crying. "Mom, can you come get me? Can you come get us?"

Elsa's heart raced. "Where are you?"

"I'm at home. Lucas took the car. He's so angry, Mom. So

angry. I just don't want to be here anymore. I can't do this anymore."

Elsa pressed her foot against the gas and raced toward the apartment building, where Mallory and Lucas had moved in together about two years before. Elsa still remembered that gorgeous day when she and Aiden had assisted Mallory in carrying a number of boxes and decorations. Mallory had never wanted to leave the island; she'd told them point-blank that her life on the Vineyard with Lucas was all she ever wanted. Then Zachery had arrived the year after, and Mallory had, for a moment, seemed the portrait of happiness.

Naturally, her father and grandfather's deaths had had a say in that happiness. Probably, it had contributed to everyday struggles at the apartment with Lucas. Add a new baby to the mix, and boom. Things were rocky. It was a recipe for disaster.

Elsa rushed up the steps to Mallory's apartment door. All she could hear was baby Zachery's wails as they rushed through the bottom of the door. Mallory had recently confessed that a number of her neighbors detested her and Lucas. Having a colic baby and screeching fights didn't help the matter. Most of the neighbors were older, divorced, and probably, whatever happened between Mallory and Lucas's walls reminded them of a life they'd all put behind them.

Elsa rapped her knuckles on the door and waited. When it seemed the noise of the knock hadn't gotten to her daughter, she instead opened the door on her own. When she stepped into the apartment, fear wrapped itself around her heart.

The place was a complete mess. Pizza boxes lined one side of the couch, all of them empty; the trash overflowed in the connecting kitchen; there were plates and bowls with half-drunk cereal and milk at various locations around the living area, including on top of the TV.

"Mal? Are you in here?"

Even as Zachery continued to wail, Mallory appeared in

the doorway between the living area and the bedroom. Her eyes were rimmed red with tears. She rushed for her mother and fell into a hug as Zachery belted out another horrendous scream.

"What happened in here?" Elsa whispered.

Mallory grimaced. "I've just spent a lot of the past few days in the bedroom with Zach."

"So that means Lucas has been sleeping out here? On the couch?"

Mallory squeezed her eyes shut and turned back toward the bedroom. Elsa took this as a yes. She followed her daughter, snaking back into the much cleaner bedroom, with its freshly washed sheets and glowing white crib, where Zachery sat, with his little hands wrapped around the wooden crib bars. His cheeks burned red with sadness as comically big tears rolled down his cheeks.

"Oh no. Baby Zach, what's the matter?" Elsa's voice lilted as she reached into the crib and drew her grandson up to her chest and shoulder. Firmly, she patted his back as he wept against her. It had been a week or two since she'd held him and the feel of his warmth filled her with a tremendous amount of longing and sadness, yet also purpose.

Mallory and Zachery needed her. Aiden's good name needed her. Cole needed her to step up and be the woman Aiden Steel had left behind.

"Is Lucas at work?" Elsa whispered as Zachery began to coo. Already, his eyelids seemed heavy; they dripped toward his cheeks as he lifted his thumb toward his lips.

Mallory shook her head. "He's on the verge of losing that job. We got into a fight earlier this afternoon about it, and he stormed out."

Elsa's heart darkened at the thought of this selfish man treating her only daughter like this. She clenched her jaw as Zachery whimpered. How horrendous was it that over the span of his life, Zachery would have to know this toxic side of Lucas as his father?

"Let's pack up everything you need and head back to Nancy's," Elsa said firmly.

Mallory's shoulders crumpled forward. "I feel so stupid and lost."

"Don't. Don't feel stupid." Elsa's chin quivered, even as she kept her eyes focused on her daughter's. "This is life, and sometimes it can deal us a bad hand, but we need to learn how to deal with it. It can smack you in the face every which way, but as long as you get back up, that's all that counts. I'm here for you every step of the way."

Zachery fell asleep in Elsa's arms a moment later. She placed him gently back in the crib and set to work, thrusting shorts and T-shirts and light jackets into Mallory's suitcase. Mallory zipped up a toiletry bag and blinked at a pad of paper there on her desk. "I should leave a note."

Mallory lifted her pen and scribbled out something unemotional. "I've gone to Mom's. Don't call or follow me. I need time to think."

Elsa carried Zachery out of the apartment while Mallory snapped the car seat into the back of Elsa's car. She placed him tenderly into the car seat and then snapped the seat belt over him. All the while, he buzzed his lips as though in his dreams, he performed some kind of song.

Once Mallory's suitcase was lodged into the back of the car, Elsa slipped into the driver's seat and watched as her daughter lifted herself into the passenger seat. Her cheeks were hollowed out; her skin was oddly the wrong color, as though she hadn't eaten properly in a while.

Still, she looked so much more like herself outside of that stupid apartment. What was it Aiden had said about the place? *"I want to buy my little girl an apartment, somewhere she'll be safe."* But Mallory and Lucas had resisted. They'd wanted to fight their own battles together.

Like most young couples, they hadn't imagined that their own battles would mostly be the ones that came between them. They hadn't imagined that their enemies would just be one another, more than everyone else.

Elsa felt so lucky that Aiden had only ever been a welcoming, loving, marvelous partner. It was the luck of the draw, maybe. Mallory certainly deserved much better than all this.

"What should we tell Nancy?" Mallory asked as they eased into the driveway.

Elsa cut the engine and furrowed her brow. "You know about Grandma Nancy's past, right?"

"Kind of."

"Well, she isn't the kind of woman to judge anything that happens to anyone else," Elsa told her. "You can tell her what happened if you want to, or you can just keep it to yourself. But just know that Nancy will support you. Janine will, too, no matter how difficult it has been for me to accept her into the family. I know she genuinely cares for us. Maybe one day, we'll love each other like real sisters."

Of course, with her own relationship with Carmella continually fraught, Elsa had tremendous difficulty imagining such a thing. Again, her most recent fight with Carmella from the previous week rushed to her mind. She hadn't seen her since. But deep down, she was grateful for it.

She wondered if Carmella had heard that Cole had won the sailing competition — the ultimate honoring of his father's memory.

She wondered if she cared at all.

Probably not.

It wasn't like Carmella had ever really stepped up into the "aunt" role, either.

When Elsa opened the front door, Nancy called out from the kitchen.

"Elsa? Is that you?"

"Sure is. I have a few guests with me."

Nancy walked in from the kitchen and beamed as Mallory carried Zachery in from the car. Mallory had left the suitcase in the back; perhaps she still wanted to pretend that this was just a normal, everyday visit.

"Look at you two. You're so beautiful," Nancy said as she beckoned for them to come farther in. "Should we set him up in the crib? He looks about as cozy as a clam."

Once Zachery slept on in the next room, Mallory, Janine, Elsa, and Nancy sat around the porch table with a bottle of chardonnay. The once-sterling day had morphed and shifted, and dark clouds brewed on the horizon and threatened to take hold of their little island.

"I love watching the storms roll in from here," Janine said softly as she dropped her head back the slightest bit. Her pony-tail swept across the top of her back. "Storms are so different in the city."

"Weren't you all the way up on the fortieth floor?" Nancy asked. "That must have been quite a show."

Janine's eyes grew shadowed, as though suddenly, she was forced to remember the unique apartment in which she had raised her two girls, far up from the grounds of Manhattan.

"It was really something. I had to pinch myself every day," Janine breathed.

After a pause, Nancy drew her hands together. "I thought we could perhaps order some pizza? Maybe have Cole over? It doesn't seem like it'll be the nicest night to be out here on the porch. We could even rent a movie if that's something you girls were interested in."

"Sounds like the type of relaxing night I need," Janine affirmed.

"Did something happen at the Lodge?" Elsa asked. She felt entirely disconnected from the place and had basically missed a whole rotation of women.

"This one woman had a meltdown today," Janine told her. "I couldn't calm her down. Nothing worked until she finally went to her suite to sleep. I'm doing everything I can. I've even changed her diet and prescribed medication. She has an acupuncture appointment with Carmella tomorrow, so we'll see if that changes anything."

"From time to time, we get women in who we can't help very well," Nancy said somberly. "It breaks me up inside, especially when they decide to go. I always want the Lodge to be an answer to all their problems. But the truth of it is, the answers have to come from within. And if we can't guide her to those answers, well..."

This dismal talk seemed a little too on the nose for what had happened with Mallory that day. When Nancy said she would head inside and order the pizza, Elsa followed her in and traced her steps to the kitchen. Once there, Nancy peered down at the takeout paper menu, which had appeared in the mailbox and gotten a lot of use since.

"Hey. Nancy?"

Nancy lifted her eyes from the menu. "What's up, honey?"

"I think Mallory might be staying with us for a little while. Just so you know."

Nancy's smile fell; her lips formed a straight line as her eyes took in the brevity of the information.

"That horrible man," she replied without even knowing the details.

Elsa nodded. "I don't know everything that happened. I just know that I don't feel good about having my girl and my grandson around him right now."

"Of course. You have to protect your own," Nancy affirmed.

"I hope it's not too much trouble for you? Having so many people here?"

"Honey, you know how I feel about that. The more, the merrier. Besides, this house is huge. Your father would have wanted them here, too. And your husband wouldn't have hesitated a single day. If he'd seen Lucas acting out, he would have picked up Mallory and Zachery himself."

Elsa's heart lifted at the mention of the goodness of Aiden's heart.

"He really was a remarkable man, wasn't he?"

Nancy studied her for a long moment. "Neal and Aiden both were, honey. We were so blessed. And now, we have to pass on those blessings to others. Don't you think?"

# Chapter Twelve

N ancy and Elsa prepared one of the guest bedrooms for Mallory's stay. Up there on the second floor, they worked in silence while making the bed, shoving the duvet into the duvet cover, putting out towels as Janine and Mallory fluttered through conversation downstairs. In a sense, it warmed Elsa's heart to hear her daughter find her way through conversation; it was true what they said about heartache. You had to "be okay" until suddenly, well, you actually were. This wasn't something Elsa had fully been able to do since Aiden and Neal's passing. She supposed that would come with time (although she dreaded this statement, as well).

"You're kidding. You know Alec Baldwin?" Mallory exclaimed downstairs as Nancy and Elsa eyed one another, grinning.

"Only through my ex-husband." Janine's voice echoed through the staircase. "He ran with a pretty wild crowd. I had to pretend I wasn't just this girl from Brooklyn — that I belonged. To be honest with you, it was exhausting."

"Still, you must have so many crazy stories," Mallory said.

Elsa caught Nancy's eye again as Nancy drew a pillowcase over a large pillow.

"Did that bother you?" Elsa asked softly.

Nancy furrowed her brow. "What?"

"You know that she lived this whole other life without you in Manhattan. After you left."

Nancy's face darkened. "Everything about our time apart bothered me. But more than anything, I bothered myself. I just couldn't get my mental health together enough for her. And so, Janine went out and conquered the world— for a little while, at least. And now, she's back. I couldn't be happier about it. Sometimes, I wake up late at night, and all these memories rush through me about our earlier days. It's like I can practically hear the angry homeless people outside, or like I know our landlord is about to come pounding on the door, demanding rent. I feel terrified, and then I have to walk myself through the many, many years since then. I relive everything. And I'm just so grateful we're here in your father's house. We're safe, and now, Mallory and Zachery are safe, too."

Elsa blinked back tears. She perched at the edge of the bed and peered into space, her hands folded. "I can't even tell you how awful that apartment looked."

"They probably feel like kids with all these adult responsibilities," Nancy returned. "That's how I felt as a young mother."

"Yes, but you were sixteen when you had Janine."

Nancy shrugged. "You never really grow up, do you? Sometimes, I feel just as young and stupid as I did back then. Sometimes, I feel even dumber."

"Stop that." Elsa's lips formed the slightest of smiles.

"It's true. But I think it's good to acknowledge our own stupidity sometimes. Nice to remember that no matter how high we get, we can always come crashing down."

The doorbell rang. Downstairs, there was the sound of

Janine and Mallory greeting the pizza deliveryman. Elsa tilted her head toward the door. "Let's go eat our weight in pizza, shall we?"

"I thought you'd never ask." Nancy hovered in the doorway to do a last once-over of the guest room. "You think Mallory will have everything she needs? We'll move the crib up here, of course."

"I think they'll be more than happy here," Elsa assured her as she placed her hand on Nancy's shoulder. "And thank you again for letting us all invade your space. First, you allow me, then Janine, and now Mallory and Zachery."

Nancy waved her hand again as tears sprang to her eyes. "You're the only one of all of us who grew up in this house. Your father left it to both of us."

It was true — with one caveat. He'd, of course, left a portion of the house and the grounds and the horses and his fortune to Carmella, despite the fact that their relationship had never flourished, especially not after the accident that happened so long ago.

But increasingly, Carmella had molded herself into something that none of them had recognized any longer. She was like a stranger to all of them.

As though Nancy could read her mind, she furrowed her brow. "You haven't spoken with Carmella this week, have you?"

Elsa shook her head as her eyes dropped toward the ground. "I've hardly managed to keep myself above water. I can't imagine what it would mean to have a normal, everyday conversation with Carmella. It always goes south, anyway."

Elsa's stomach filled with stones as she realized, yet again, that she hadn't spoken to Nancy at all about the letter she had received or about the potential lawsuit against Aiden's estate — her estate. Just now, she wanted bright laughter; she wanted bad reality television; she wanted to bicker with her new stepsister and her daughter and her son and her stepmother about which movie to watch to pass the time together. The pizza was terrifically gooey, heaping with toppings, and the light from the windows morphed from post-storm buttermilk to orange as time ticked them ever-more toward evening.

It was a remarkable night, if only because, for a little while, there was so much love to go around that Elsa was allowed to forget about all the other stuff on her plate.

Maybe they'd all be able to.

* * *

The following afternoon, Elsa stepped out of the office and into the blinding light of yet another smoldering July sun. After the calm of the evening, another storm had rolled over their rock of the island and torn several branches from beach-side trees. Even now, some of the Lodge gardeners continued to clean up the wreckage. Probably, in a few days' time, they would have a bonfire out near the sand.

Frequently, they had their Lodge guests attend bonfires, where they wrote out various things they wanted to "let go of" onto slips of paper and tossed them in the flickering flames. Sometimes, the women told one another what they wrote — about their ex-husband who had left them in a lurch, or the sorrow over their loss of a friendship, or some other hurdle that made their insides tie up in knots.

Elsa had never performed the ritual with them. She had never felt that she'd wanted anything in her life to depart. Even as a child, she had longed to hold each and every one of her stuffed animals in her arms as she'd fallen asleep. She hadn't wanted one of them to think she thought less of them or even considered giving them away to some charity. She had even tried to make sure she played with each of them equally — a trying task and one that made her an increasingly anxious child. "Your stuffed animals know you love them," her mother, Tina, had told her once as she had fallen asleep. "You don't have to feel guilty about your love for each of them."

Carmella sauntered from the parking lot. She wore thick Chanel black sunglasses and carried a sloshing iced coffee. She looked fit; as her long, lean legs showed from halfway down her dress. She gave no smile to Elsa, and Elsa lent nothing in return.

"Hey, there." Elsa stopped before she got into her own car.

"Are you heading out?"

"Yep."

"It's pretty early. I haven't seen you around very often."

Elsa gave a lackluster shrug. How could she possibly explain everything that had happened to this creature before her? The woman was essentially a stranger.

"I hired Jennifer Conrad to do a lot of the social media for the time being, and I've managed to fit in all relevant meetings between other things," Elsa told her. Immediately afterward, Elsa cursed herself. She didn't have to prove anything to Carmella.

"Huh. Well. It's a beautiful day out here. Enjoy it. I have another four hours of clients till I can pack it in." Carmella then slurped up her coffee and rushed back toward the door, where she ducked into the air-conditioned room.

Elsa seethed with resentment as she popped her car door open and slid into the front seat. All the way back to the house, her heart performed a tap dance across her diaphragm. "She has some kind of nerve," she muttered to herself.

Neal had always known what to say when Elsa's anger toward Carmella had taken new heights. No, he hadn't always agreed with Carmella and often had grown red-faced with similar rage, which he never verbally expressed to either of them.

"You girls just have very different ways of looking at the

world," he'd said frequently. "And you're both incredibly empathetic to everyone, except one another. It's a sad thing to watch. But isn't that what sisters do? You wage war on one another without seeing your similarities. Try to see them, Elsa. Try to see the good in her, too."

Just as she had long ago in conversation with her father, Elsa tried to drum up a list of all the things she liked or, for better words, loved about her sister.

"She is so clever," she tried as she clutched the steering wheel harder. "She's the top ten of her class and much braver than I ever was. She was always clambering up to the tallest branch of that tree by the water. I hated when she did that. What else? What else?" Elsa scrunched her nose as she stabbed the fob to open the garage door. "She doesn't need people the way I do. She's self-sufficient. How wonderful would it be to live life like that? To go to sleep and wake up without this heavy loneliness?"

But then, her psyche piped up with its own opinion that just because Elsa didn't think Carmella got lonely didn't mean she sometimes didn't get lonely. Everyone did, didn't they?

And it was especially true if what their father had said was really correct, that they were more alike than either of them knew.

Elsa stepped upstairs. Mallory had the day off, and the sound of her soothing, sweet singing voice eased beneath the crack in the guest bedroom. It seemed that since Zachery's arrival to the old homestead the previous day, he had hardly cried at all.

She was just so glad they were both out of that place until she and Lucas had resolved their issues. They had to make amends. They were engaged, after all, and just had a child together. Elsa knew deep down that they would make their way back to one another; she hoped anyway.

Already, Mallory had texted her mother to say that she planned to tell Lucas it was over between them.

> MALLORY: I'm ready for a new start. I don't know why, but I feel it in my gut. It's time for something else.

Elsa paused at her closet door and thought back to what Mallory had said. This concept of "new start" was certainly alluring, if not intoxicating. It seemed that everywhere she looked that others were on the verge of their own. Mallory had jumped ship; Janine had run away from Manhattan; Nancy had thrown herself totally back into the Lodge. Only Elsa dragged her feet.

Operating on some kind of strange reflex, Elsa swept through her various outfits, her long skirts, her slacks, her work suits until she finally found, toward the back, her riding uniform. She stripped down to her bra and panties and then donned the outfit. In the mirror, she shifted this way, then that, and gave herself a pointed smile. She looked slender, her muscles toned and powerful — the direct antithesis of everything she felt. How was it possible that you could exude something you didn't feel? She supposed that was a kind of magic or maybe just an illusion.

Once outside, she donned her riding cap and headed straight for the stables. They'd kept horses since she had been a little girl, and in the years leading up to the accident that had changed everything, she'd been quite the rider. She had won several competitions as a youth and then as a young teen, and she'd even taught lessons for a time. In her adult years, she hadn't been particularly keen to allow her children to ride, as she'd been terrified something might happen.

"I just can't get the image out of my head," she'd told Aiden as tears had streamed down her cheeks.

Of course, this image had everything to do with her little brother. With Colton — the inspiration behind Cole's name.

He'd been gone so long that she hardly remembered his face.

Only some amount of love and a whole lot of fear remained.

Nancy still rode frequently. Elsa had often seen her as she'd rushed across the beach; her horse's hooves kicked out sand behind them as his mane flowed freely with the ocean winds. To Elsa, the view of Nancy on horseback was one of absolute freedom.

Yet, for whatever reason, she hadn't been able to grasp her own version of that. Not until now, that was.

The chestnut-colored beauty toward the far end of the stables dipped his nose over the wooden stall as though he had known all along Elsa would come — as though he'd never doubted it for a second.

# Chapter Thirteen

Elsa's father had purchased the grounds on which he'd built his moderately-sized mansion a few years prior to his eldest child's birth. This meant that, since Elsa had first wobbled forward on her first step, or swam in the sea, or ridden on a horse — this land had been her world, her universe. It had seemed incredible that there had even been any property outside what they owned at the house. The rolling hills, which dipped into the surrounding forest, which then filtered out across the blissfully white, sandy beaches — it all belonged to her. And as her horse stretched its legs out toward the trails beyond, she felt a powerful force. It was as though Neal raced on horseback directly behind her. It was as though his soul rushed through the waters and swept through the sea breezes.

She didn't feel so alone when she was riding.

The property on which Neal had built the house was seventy-five acres, and it stretched all the way eastward toward the Katama Lodge itself. Elsa lifted the reins of her horse, a light suggestion to the animal to pause, and together they gazed out across the rolling greens and the flash of white sands. In the distance, out across the Atlantic Ocean, a sailboat coasted across the waves. Elsa marveled at it all. How many afternoons of the previous year had she spent inside, feeling the tremendous weight of her own life?

Nothing felt as heavy out there on horseback— not time nor memory nor the fear of what would come next.

Elsa's horse trotted and then clopped across the sands. Elsa found herself rolling through thoughts easily. For the first time, she recognized that she was separate from those thoughts — that they came and went as they willed, and that in their wake, she remained there on horseback. She was okay.

*What was it about Carmella that irritated me so much? Is it really because of everything that happened with Karen? Or is it rooted in what happened with Colton?*

*Or did it begin much earlier? I remember once, when I was maybe six or seven, I came into my room, and she'd yanked the head off one of my dolls. I told Dad she was a little monster, and he said that she was probably just jealous that all my toys took up my time when I should have been playing with Carmella.*

*I suppose, in a way, we always mess one another up — no matter how much we try not to.*

*Still, the past thirty years haven't been easy for her. I wonder if I should give her some kind of slack?*

*Then again, she hardly looks at me when I'm around. I can't even imagine what that conversation would look like. "Hey, Carmella! Why don't we grab lunch? Just the two of us?" She would probably scoff, or have me committed to an insane asylum, or say something so ridiculously cruel that I would begin to question every single thing about myself — from the wrinkles around my eyes to the way I dress, to...*

Elsa's thoughts stirred lightly. She was surprised to find herself so hyper-focused on Carmella, especially with everything currently swirling around Aiden's case and Mallory and

Lucas's breakup. For the previous year, Nancy suggested that Elsa find a therapist to deal with some of the trauma in her life. Still, Elsa hadn't found the words to even speak to herself about it. She had imagined herself on the therapist's couch, twiddling her thumbs until the clock ran out. "Can I go? I have so much to do." It would have probably been like that.

The horse shot through the trees. Elsa loved the immediate ease of the forest, the cool air as it rushed past her skin like water. Light filtered through the treetops and cast strange shadows across the horse's mane. Her shoulders hung loose as she experimented with her breathing: in, out. In, out. She'd heard Nancy's instructions on breathing in her yoga classes and massage studio; perhaps there really was something to all that focused breathing. Perhaps the Lodge really did have a hand in all that "healing" she advertised day in, day out.

How had she become such a cynic? She thought then. She supposed it hadn't been her original status. She'd once believed in so much magic. She'd once believed in—

But suddenly, there was the flash of a small animal as it cut across the trail. What was it? A squirrel? Perhaps a chipmunk? The horse whinnied frantically and burst up from the trail. Elsa clung to the reins as best as her heart jumped into her throat. But the horse remained tossed back, and Elsa wasn't the strong rider she'd once been. She was bucked from her saddle and landed against the pine-cone-laden soil off to the side. She cried out in pain. A sound echoed through the tops of the trees as her horse raced all the way back toward the estate.

Elsa blinked up from the ground. The shock had overtaken her so that her eyes flashed with strange bolts of light, and her head rang like a bell. She'd never been tossed off a horse before, but the memory of her brother's accident made her quake with terror.

It hadn't gone the right way with him.

But then again, why had she been okay now, when he'd —

Well, it did her no good to ask such things of the universe. Could she feel everything? Was she paralyzed? No, she could feel her fingers, and she could wiggle her toes. She clenched her eyes tight and counted to ten as though she would have the bravery to stand again once she reached it.

Seven — eight — nine ...

The rushing flash of something like feet across the brush, through the pines. "Hello? Is someone there?" A man's voice rang out, brimming with fear. "I heard someone scream?"

Elsa buzzed her lips with resentment. One saving grace in all of this had been that she was all right, and nobody had witnessed such an embarrassment.

"Hello?" the voice called out again.

Elsa latched onto whatever strength she had left to emit the slightest of sounds. "I'm here." She sounded pitiful.

Suddenly, the man appeared on the path just beyond the crest of the hill. He was broad-shouldered, prominent, with dark hair and bright green eyes. He wore a white V-neck T-shirt, crisp and perhaps new, along with a pair of sweatpants and a Boston Red Sox baseball cap. Elsa blinked at the sight of him as her stomach stirred with a mix of shame and — admittedly, attraction. Whoever that man was, he probably made some woman very, very happy.

"Elsa?"

He was no more than five feet away when he said it. Elsa scrunched her nose, placed her elbows against the soil, and drew herself up the slightest bit. Her helmet was crooked, and it had tipped over her right ear. She probably looked so silly. In a moment, her eyes found his.

"Mr. Holland. Hello."

It was the handsome attorney from the law office of Susan Sheridan. Their eyes connected for a long moment as both took in the full sight of each other. Elsa's nostrils flared as she allowed embarrassment to swallow her whole.

"Are you okay?" Bruce asked. "I was running on the side of the road, and I heard someone scream, and well, I was terrified."

Elsa turned her head slowly, tenderly, to investigate the area of the forest where her horse had run off. "There was a squirrel or something that spooked my horse. It's my fault. I hadn't taken him out in a long time. Probably, he just wasn't used to it."

Bruce knelt. He still looked enormous, even so low to the ground. It was clearly not a stance he often took, as it looked terribly uncomfortable.

"You didn't hurt your neck or your head?"

"No. I don't think so."

"Promise? Because I can call an ambulance right this minute. Actually, I'd feel better about it."

Elsa groaned. "Please, don't do that. I can't bear any more hospital rooms."

Bruce nodded knowingly. Elsa remembered with a jolt that he'd lost his wife, too. And what was a hospital room if not space to reckon with the demise of those you loved or yourself?

"Let's just take it really slow," Bruce said.

Elsa longed to joke that he sounded like a scared man on a first date: *let's take this slow, okay? I like you, but I'm just not sure.* She and Aiden, of course, hadn't been like that; they'd jumped forward into life together as though the world behind them had been on fire.

Bruce placed his hand on Elsa's upper back and instructed her to stop if even one little pang of pain shot through her. Elsa lifted up higher so that she sat with her legs extended out.

"I'm dusty," she said lightly.

"You're a woman of the woods," Bruce returned with a laugh.

"I'm sure you mean that as a compliment."

"Absolutely." Bruce's eyes were electric, far brighter green than they'd been back at the law office.

When Elsa stood upright, Bruce made her wiggle her arms and legs and she stretched out her back for any signs of damage.

"How old are you, exactly?" Bruce asked her.

"Forty-five."

"And you seriously just got up from a horseback riding accident? Are you made of rubber?" Bruce asked. "If that had happened to me, I would be in about five pieces right now."

Elsa laughed. "When I was a girl, they taught us how to fall in our horseback riding lessons. I guess all the training kicked back in, and I just went loose."

"And your horse? Back where he came from?"

"Probably," Elsa returned. She glanced back across the trail, where Bruce had come from. "You run out on that main road? Sounds dangerous. You should really run in these woods."

Bruce shrugged. "It's private property, isn't it?"

"It's ours. My father's."

"I know."

Elsa swallowed the lump in her throat. Why had she grown so jittery all of a sudden?

"It was so wonderful that you were so close— saving me all over again."

"I don't live that far from here. I've gotten addicted to running the past few weeks. I find it calms me down a little bit. It really takes my mind off other things."

"That's the game, isn't it? Occupying your mind enough so you can continue to live," Elsa returned.

Again, they held one another's gaze. Sea breeze fluttered through the treetops and cast the branches to and fro. It felt remarkable to be the only two souls in those woods, as though they'd been allowed a secret portal into another world, one for just the two of them.

"Do you want to walk back to the house with me?" Elsa asked suddenly. The words were a surprise to her. They had flowed out of her mouth without even a thought. "I want to check on the horse and maybe grab you a glass of lemonade?"

Bruce agreed to walk her back. They eased alongside one another and stepped through the trails. Their feet crunched across the previous fall's dead leaves; sticks and branches clipped apart beneath them. A sparrow fluttered onto a nearby tree and peered at them earnestly as though it demanded something of them.

"I can't believe I went so long without nature like this," Bruce admitted. "All those years in Boston. I knew something was missing. I didn't know it was the sea, the wind, animals, and just nature in general."

"Ah, you turned into a city guy. You turned your back on us islanders and went off and experienced all that culture," Elsa teased. "Now you think you can just come back and enjoy our wildlife? Think again, sir."

He laughed outright at that. "I know. My wife was such a city girl. She always called me an island bumpkin."

"Bumpkin! That's quite a term of endearment," Elsa teased.

Bruce's eyes seemed far away, perhaps latched to his memories. "I took her here a few times. I loved her to pieces, but she never had much to say about wildlife. I think one too many pigeons had pooped on her in her home of Boston, you know?"

"Ah. Once nature turns on you, you can never go back."

"Is that how you feel about your horse?" Bruce asked.

"Nah. He was spooked. I was spooked. We're even."

Bruce contemplated this for a moment.

"What?" Elsa asked. The look that brewed on his face captivated her.

"Nothing. I just would think that most women — most

people, I mean—would be terrified to get back on the horse after that."

Elsa felt the pressing weight of all her stories — of Colton's death, of Carmella's anger, of the hours and hours of conversation she'd had with her father while he had ridden on horseback beside her.

"Riding horses is a part of my soul, I guess. It always has been," Elsa breathed. "I guess it's true what they say. Sometimes, the things that you love the most jump up and bite you. If you really love them — whether it's riding horses or sailing boats or racing bulls through the streets of Spain, it's something that stays with you forever."

"Nice reference," Bruce affirmed.

"Whatever it is you love, you have to love it despite its faults. Right?"

Bruce gave a light shrug. "I think you're right. However, I've never heard it said that way. It's almost poetic."

Elsa chuckled as her father's house appeared through the trees. "I'm no poet. I'm just making everything up as I go along."

"Isn't everyone?" Bruce's grin widened as they stepped out from the last line of the trees to discover Elsa's horse; he stood and kicked one of his front hooves against the grass and shook out his mane beautifully.

It was almost as though he demanded, *where have you been? I've been waiting for you.*

# Chapter Fourteen

Mallory propped Zachery up in his baby chair and cooed at him as Zachery buzzed his little pink lips. His eyes danced with excitement as his mother dropped the tiniest of spoons into pea mash and whispered, "Are you ready for the airplane, Zachery?"

Elsa hovered near the bay window with a glass of water in hand. She was freshly showered, and her hair had curled beautifully down her back from the dense humidity the late July afternoon had offered her. Only an hour before, Bruce had departed and struck out again on his run. She had watched him for a bit too long as he had stretched his long legs toward the road and then disappeared from sight.

"You look pretty, Mom," Mallory said as Zachery clopped on his pea mash and smacked his palms across the top of the baby chair.

"Oh? Thanks." Elsa twirled a finger through her curl and shifted her weight. "Cole said he's out sailing today. I thought I would head down to the docks later. Say hi."

Mallory's smile faltered just the slightest bit. "That sounds fun." Her eyes reflected a strange mix of curiosity and sadness. "Any reason? You were never particularly fond of those sailor guys."

Elsa hadn't yet explained Aiden's predicament to her daughter. Elsa made sure that Cole only knew the bare minimum — that various members of the sailing community and otherwise had decided to drag his father's name through the mud. This was the reason Elsa wanted to journey down there. She wanted to eavesdrop. She wanted to learn all she could. She couldn't bear the thought that they could just guzzle beer after beer and throw around horrific rumors of Aiden that just weren't true.

She had to put up a fight.

"I know, but that world means so much to Cole, and it would have meant so much to your dad," Elsa offered Mallory now. "I'm sure you could come over if you'd like to. Maybe Nancy or Janine would babysit?"

Mallory shook her head sadly. "I have too much to do, I think. I want to apply for a few more jobs. Get something more stable, like a nine-to-five."

Elsa tilted her head. "You didn't mention that."

"Yeah. I've been thinking about it a lot. I think now, with Lucas out of the picture, it's time for me to grow up."

"You know, we really need a secretary at the Lodge," Elsa informed her. "And I would love to have you on staff. You're reliable. And I know the Lodge already means a lot to you."

Mallory's eyes brightened. This was a surprise to Elsa, as Mallory had traditionally all been about "forging her own path" and "striking out from her family." Perhaps that was what growing up was all about. Realizing that really, you couldn't do it all on your own.

"I'll talk to Nancy about it when she gets home," Mallory offered excitedly. "But I can't imagine a better gig."

"It's a family affair!" Elsa's heart leaped into her throat. "Your grandfather would be so thrilled."

Elsa buzzed with this news as she drove over to Edgartown Harbor. It was nearly seven thirty, and the island resembled a painting. A soft orange light glowed across window panes with streaks of light clouds through the sky. Then she had a full view of the harbor, with its tilting sailboats, its reflecting water, and its yonder Edgartown lighthouse, which had once drawn sailors and whalers home.

Elsa parked a few blocks from the docks and then headed back. The breeze caught her black dress and whipped it around her knees. As she sauntered forward, several men marched past and actually dared to check her out! Their eyes scanned her chest, the cinch of her waist, and the length of her calves. She felt remarkable, electric — nothing like the woman who'd fallen from horseback only that afternoon. Perhaps her luck was changing. Perhaps Bruce Holland was a part of that luck.

Not that she cared for anyone beyond her husband, of course.

But she did buzz with something. Expectation? New hope? She wasn't entirely sure.

She spotted Cole on the far end of one of the docks. He was bent down as he tied up his sailboat, which creaked against the wooden slats of the dock beneath him. When he stood, he placed his hand over his eyes to shield the sun. He then spotted his mother and waved a sturdy hand.

"Hey, you." When he approached, she hugged him tightly. She tried again to shove out all thought of his resemblance to his father. It wasn't fair to him to drum up such sorrow. Not then. "How was it out there today?"

"Not bad," Cole said as he stepped back. "Although I'm glad you came down. I heard a few of the guys talking about Dad again this morning before I headed out and—" His nostrils flared, as though his anger disallowed him to say anything else.

"We'll get to the bottom of this," Elsa told him.

"They've all headed to the bar," Cole said as he tilted his head. "A few of my buddies already have a table. Probably, those other idiots are already too drunk to even recognize you're Aiden Steel's wife."

"I take it they aren't as committed to long days at sea as you are?"

"I think they're in the sailing game for a different reason." Cole imitated drinking a large beer as he rolled his eyes back in his head.

Elsa couldn't help it. Despite the anger that permeated through her mind, she chuckled at Cole's clownish behavior.

"These idiots won't be the ones to do this to your father. No way in hell," Elsa affirmed.

The bar was the traditional watering hole for many of Martha's Vineyard sailors. As such, even now, at eight in the evening, it was already rowdy with red-faced and tanned men drinking countless pints of beers as fast as they could, flirting with the waitresses, and demanding specific songs to be played on the speaker system. The bar began in a small building and then burst onto the sands along the water. Electric lights were hung, and they glowed softly as the day's sky faded into the evening around them.

Elsa greeted Cole's friends, most of whom she had known since Cole had been six or seven years old. That was typical of the Vineyard—people stuck to one another for life.

"Marty. Catherine. Wally. Good to see you," Elsa said as Cole disappeared into the crowd to grab them both drinks. "Did you all sail today?"

They all nodded, then chuckled a little, knowing it was a silly question but didn't want to be rude. Of course, they'd sailed that day. Was there even anything else to do?

Cole returned and placed a glass of wine in front of Elsa. He then sat and pointed a finger low and leftward as he muttered, "They're over there. The guys from the sailing race. They're the same ones who were talking about Dad this morning, too."

Elsa recognized the salt-and-pepper-haired man and his friend, the blond guy. They sat at one end of a long table, alongside three women who seemed to be in their early- to mid-twenties. One of them had long, flowing red hair, while the other two were blond. Each seemed to have an extra six inches of leg than the rest of the female population and all of them had highlighted their cleavage in ways that weren't exactly church friendly.

"I see they brought their daughters," Elsa said with a crooked smile.

Cole rolled his eyes. "Oh my God, Mom. Really."

"I just — ugh. Guys like these. I never understood why your father even gave them the time of day," Elsa returned.

"They're sailors. Dad was in it for the sport, not for them," Cole pointed out. "Not like they have anything in common besides sailing, anyway." Cole added, "And if you think for a minute Dad ever hung out with women like that while he was here..."

Elsa's cheeks grew warm. In truth, she had never imagined anything like that. She bit hard on the inside of her cheek as her eyes met Cole's. "I know your father was a good, honest, and upstanding man. It's part of the reason I married him in the first place, and it's why I'm here right now. I want the world to remember him as he was, and not how these jerks want to pretend he was."

Cole nodded firmly. "Good."

Elsa wanted to tell him then how she admired the fire behind everything he did. He was powerful, strong like his father.

But there were times when compliments from your mother

were okay, and then there were other times. It would have to come later.

"You don't know those guys' names, do you?" Elsa asked.

Cole shook his head. "No."

"Or the girls with them?"

"No. Never seen them before," Cole admitted.

Elsa sipped her wine, a chardonnay that seemed overly sweet, which was almost fitting for the bar since it didn't have the best wine selection. She kept one eye on the sailors and their younger women and one eye on her table, Cole's friends, to attempt not to raise suspicion. She was there to eavesdrop and gather any pertinent information she could, and she didn't even bother to tell Cole her plan beforehand.

It was a natural thing that girls went to the bathroom together. As if on cue, when one of the blond girls at the far table stood, both of the other girls stood along with her. They flashed their hair behind their overly sharp shoulders and then sauntered toward the women's restroom.

This was Elsa's sign.

Cole was in the midst of a heavy conversation with Marty, who disagreed with him about one of the recent new sailing regulations. Elsa muttered to Cole that she would be right back, and he just nodded, totally distracted. She grabbed her purse and rushed toward the bathroom door, which still squeaked back and forth from the girls' entrance.

The bathroom wasn't as bad as the rest of the place. A bright red couch was situated alongside a floor-to-ceiling mirror, which seemed antique and special, save for the graffiti written across the side that read: ZACH AND TONYA FOREVER. All three of the girls had stationed themselves at the three sinks. They were in the midst of their traditional grooming patterns like touching up their lipstick, spraying on more perfume, and tending to their mascara in a way that seemed entirely fashionable and overdone.

Elsa waited near the couch. The girls were quiet. She felt sure the gossip would spin up soon, but maybe, she had to coax it the slightest bit.

"Can you imagine loving Zach so much that you write about him on the mirror?" Elsa said suddenly as she pointed at the graffiti.

To her surprise, the one red-haired girl turned around. She gestured with the mascara wand and said, "We know Tonya. She's an idiot."

The other blond girl off to the right burst into laughter. "Zach knocked her up, and then she didn't know what to do, so she moved back in with her mom. She's taking night classes while Zach is running around with this other girl now. Chloe."

Elsa's heart grew heavy at the sudden onslaught of this story. Still, she had to keep her gossip-ready face fresh. "Wow. Did you see that coming?"

"Absolutely," the red-haired girl said. She seemed to be their leader. "Tonya was head over heels for Zach. We told her to play the game like us. We told her not to mess around with twentysomethings, you know? We went to school with guys our own age. We should know firsthand what idiots they are."

"Totally," one of the blond girls said.

"Wow. Things have really changed since I was younger," Elsa said.

One of the blond girls caught her eye in the mirror. "You don't look old at all. What are you? Thirty-five?"

"Forty-five, actually," Elsa corrected as she swung a curl over her ear.

The red-haired girl whipped around again to fully inspect her as though she was a prized pig at the fair. "Really! No way. What kind of moisturizer do you use?"

"Are you into retinol?" one of the blond girls demanded.

The red-haired girl chuckled lightly. "Sorry. We shouldn't

pepper you with so many questions. Do you need the mirror? Girls, scoot over."

The three girls wrapped themselves around two of the sinks while Elsa slid up to the one off to the left. She reached into her purse and drew out a stick of lipstick, which she propped delicately against her lower lip. A strange idea brewed up in the back of Elsa's mind as she forced herself to entertain it.

"When I was around your age, I did have a brief affair with an older man," Elsa tried. "It was such a dream come true. He took me out on his sailboat, and we raced all over the ocean. I had all these dreams that he would take me across the world with him."

The red-haired girl arched an eyebrow. "And he didn't?"

Elsa shrugged. "I had to be here. I had responsibilities on the island."

"Yes, but if he had provided for you, all those responsibilities would have floated away," the girl pointed out.

Elsa furrowed her brow with feigned confusion. The red-haired girl stabbed her mascara wand into its container and tightened it up.

"Let's put it this way. If you had played your cards right, you could have been like me and Gretchen and Rhea here," the blonde continued. "We met those men out there on a dating service in the city. Not even one of us could pay our rent on time. Remember that, girls?"

"God, it was awful," Gretchen affirmed as she adjusted her bra strap beneath her skintight dress.

"So it's like a call service?" Elsa asked.

Gretchen shook her head. "No. We're more than that. We're companions for these men. Friends with, you know, a few extra benefits."

The blonde giggled. "And in return, they give us everything we need. And they take us all over the world. This is our only job, to travel, to stay beautiful, and to keep them happy."

Elsa was mesmerized. The world really had changed or at least revealed its true self to her, just a forever-islander who'd hardly spent a day off it.

"So those guys are pretty successful, then?" Elsa dabbed still more lipstick across her lower lip. Did she have other makeup in her bag? She wasn't sure. She had to make this technique last.

"Absolutely," Rhea said. "They live between here and New York, but they travel all over the world. God, remember that apartment they took us to in Paris?"

The red-haired girl murmured yes as she lifted her eyebrows high to fix her own lipstick.

"Too bad I missed out on all that when I was younger," Elsa breathed with fake regret.

"You really did," Gretchen said sadly.

"I think I recognize those men," Elsa said. "From sailing contests around here."

"Yes. Carlson Montague and Peterson Hughes," the blond girl affirmed. "They're quite prosperous businessmen. They've worked on Wall Street and... just between you and me, they have a number of offshore accounts. If you know what I mean."

Elsa's heart jumped into her throat. She was careful to deliver a sneaky grin, one meant to illustrate just how "in the know" and "cool" she was with what the three girls and their men were up to.

But her mind raced in a million different directions. After all, Carlson Montague was the name of the man who now attempted to sue her estate and destroy her husband's good name.

And it was clear that he was up to no good.

Elsa just had no idea how on earth she could possibly prove this to anyone.

The girls finished up their looks with the last blasts of perfume. They bid Elsa goodbye with bright smiles, then clacked back out to the beach bar. Elsa gripped either side of the sink and heaved at her reflection.

"Aiden. What the heck were you doing messed up with Carlson Montague? And why is he after you?"

# Chapter Fifteen

E lsa spent the following morning, afternoon, and early evening in her office at the Lodge. She had a number of meetings to catch up with, about a thousand emails to arrange, and beyond that, she'd agreed to give Mallory an introduction to her new position as Lodge secretary, which Nancy had agreed to wholeheartedly. Around noon, her beautiful daughter stepped into her office in one of Elsa's own business suits; her chin held high as she said, "All right. I'm ready for training."

Mallory took to the work easily. She greeted incoming guests with a warm smile, entered their information into the computer, showed each woman to her separate suite, and gave them each their individualized schedule — one that had already been highlighted and put together by Janine, the doctor on-site. Each time it was quiet at the desk, Mallory rushed over to Elsa's office and did a little dance in the doorway.

"I just can't believe I get to work here!" she squealed. "I still remember all those times you brought me and Cole and Alexie here as kids. We were so amazed with the Lodge. It was like our playhouse."

"I know. You always got into so much trouble," Elsa said. "Your father had to run after you once when you tried to duck into the spa. All those women without clothing on, and a little six-year-old girl about to ruin their calm afternoon."

Mallory laughed. "I just loved the steam. It reminded me of when the fog would roll in. Almost like magic."

"It's still like magic. The kind of magic that can take away your problems." Elsa flashed her daughter a genuine smile.

Between conversations with Mallory and other staff members, Elsa continued to ponder what the girls from the previous night at the bar had said about Carlson Montague. Cole had said he'd heard of a number of "escorts" in recent years; it was apparently very popular with girls his age who wanted older men to pay for their college and rent and other expenditures.

"But what does this have to do with your father?" Elsa had asked.

"Dad didn't have an escort," Cole had returned, bristling.

"I know that, Cole. He wouldn't have had the time, anyway. You remember. He almost always wanted to cook dinner. I remember because he frequently burned it, which is why our house always smelled like burnt food and then the takeout when he had to order afterward," Elsa had said as she squeezed Cole's elbow.

Still, the whole thing was curious. It felt as though they had a number of puzzle pieces, but none of them seemed to add up to a relevant puzzle.

When Elsa arrived home that evening, she found the driveway full of familiar vehicles. From the porch overlooking the water came a number of voices, wild giggles, and the occasional screech from the baby. Once inside, she headed upstairs, changed into a summer dress, then appeared at the doorway between the kitchen and the porch to find a number of beautiful faces — Cole and Mallory and Zachery, plus Nancy and Janine, along with her daughters, Maggie and Alyssa, who were visiting.

And there, seated directly next to Nancy, was Carmella.

Elsa hadn't seen Carmella since their recent tiff. Her smile faltered immediately, even as Mallory stepped up to deliver her mother a glass of wine and a bright, "Hello! Nancy wanted to celebrate my first day. I had no idea so many people would be here."

Elsa forced herself to smile for her daughter and accepted the glass. "You did beautifully, honey. I'm so glad you're on the team."

Alyssa waved from the table. "Hi, Aunt Elsa!" she said.

"Aunt Elsa, hello!" Maggie chimed in.

"I had no idea you girls were coming in from the city," Elsa said. Her voice felt strained, as though it belonged to someone else. All the while, she felt Carmella's eyes boring into her skull.

What the heck was she doing here? She didn't participate in family dinners.

"We wanted to surprise Mom," Maggie said. "She's been working so dang hard."

Janine blushed as she sipped her wine. "Elsa, Nancy, and I have worked ourselves silly at that Lodge. It's true. But I have to say, I go to bed happy every single night. It's incredible, helping the women who come through there."

"I feel the same way," Carmella piped in then. "It's why I missed it so much while we were closed."

Elsa's heart dropped. Again, resentment filled the space between them. She detested the fact that Carmella hadn't wanted to be closed at all. As though she hadn't needed any kind of grieving period for their father because it hadn't mattered to her at all.

"Oh, Maggie, you have to let Carmella take a look at your shoulder," Janine said then.

"Acupuncture, right?" Maggie said to Carmella.

"Yes. It's kind of like magic." Carmella's smile widened. "I fell in love with it when I was in my early twenties, traveling through the southwest. My stepmother first introduced me to it, though."

"Grandma?" Alyssa asked, furrowing her brow.

"No, no. My other stepmother," Carmella returned. "She and my father divorced before he and Nancy got together. Anyway, she taught me all about the healing powers of acupuncture."

Elsa's nostrils flared. She could feel the resentment beaming off Carmella's words. Carmella loved to bring up Karen, especially around Elsa, as she knew how much Elsa hated Karen. Karen had been her wicked stepmother. Karen had destroyed the fabric of their family, and it had been up to Elsa and Neal to pick the pieces back up and stitch them together again. Carmella hadn't wanted to be included in that patchwork process.

"Well, wherever you picked it up, you're remarkable at it," Janine continued. Her smile never faltered. "The other day, when I left your office, I felt like my arms and legs were made of literal jelly. Girls, you have to try it. I felt like I didn't have a single care in the world. And you know that, well, I have had a few cares... especially lately."

"That reminds me!" Alyssa cried. "How is Henry doing?"

Janine's cheeks brightened pink. "Oh, girls, I told you. Whatever that is, it's going to go as slow as molasses, or not at all. I'll let you know if there's anything exciting to know about."

Still, Janine gave the sneakiest of smiles as Carmella swatted her over the knee.

"She's keeping stuff from you, Maggie and Alyssa," Carmella said conspiratorially. "I saw Henry slinking around the back of the Lodge the other day. He was hunting for someone."

"Mom!" Alyssa cried.

"Mom, you're acting like a teenager. Just tell us what's up!" Maggie blurted.

Elsa's stomach ballooned with annoyance. She carried her wine in from the porch and stepped into the kitchen, where she gripped the counter hard and focused on her breath.

First of all, when had Carmella and Janine become such good friends? Elsa and Carmella had never teased one another the way Carmella had just teased Janine, and the way Janine had complimented Carmella had been completely outside of Elsa's comfort zone.

But beyond that, Elsa hated that Carmella had just "exposed" Janine and Henry's little, not-so-complicated, very sweet affair. Why did Carmella dig into other people's business like that? Why did she think she had the right?

Someone entered the house. The screen door slammed shut, and then, there was the dramatic *clack-clack* of a pair of heels that echoed off the walls. Everyone else at the house was barefoot; why did Carmella think it was okay to wear some city-girl heels across the wooden slats of the porch?

"I can see it written all over your face." Carmella's voice was sour.

Elsa remained facing the back wall. She wanted nothing to do with whatever fight now brewed between them.

"You hate that I'm getting along with them—with Janine and Nancy."

Elsa's nostrils flared. "That's ridiculous."

"You can't understand why they would ever like me."

"That's also ridiculous. Everyone likes you. You're beautiful, Carmella." Elsa's voice was mocking. She sounded childish, even to herself. She resented this, too.

Carmella clacked the rest of the way to the dishwasher,

which she pulled open forcefully. One by one, she slid in plate after plate, none of which looked so dirty.

"You really should have just washed them in the sink," Elsa returned.

"Right. You live here, now. You make the rules. I forgot," Carmella said.

"It's just a waste of space and water," Elsa said.

Carmella scoffed. "Don't pretend that this is about wasting water."

Elsa rolled her eyes back. "I can't believe you hold that woman up so much."

"What are you talking about?"

"Karen. I can't believe you talk about her like she was some kind of goddess."

Carmella bristled. She crossed her arms over her chest as her nostrils flared. "I shouldn't be angry with you. I know your memory is very selective."

"Oh, honey. It's not selective at all," Elsa blurted. "I remember everything she did to you, to me, and especially to Dad."

"She was only kind to me, and you hated that," Carmella returned. "Now that I'm also building a better relationship with Nancy, you're jealous all over again. It's like we're teenagers. How gross."

"You're the one acting like a teenager," Elsa seethed through clenched teeth. "I'm a — a wife and a mother and a —"

Carmella clucked her tongue. "That's been your saving grace this whole time, right? Just because you did everything right, every step of the way, you were allowed to pretend that you weren't as messed up as me. Well, I have news for you."

Suddenly, the screen door smacked open and shut again. A shadow fell over the sisters as Nancy rushed inside. Her face was stricken; her eyes were electric, as though they could spit flames.

"What on earth are you girls talking about?" she demanded.

All the color drained immediately from Elsa's cheeks. Nancy had never spoken to her like this before — like a mother might to a child.

"Do you know that we are all out there on the porch, trying to have a nice time, as a family, while you girls are in here trying to tear one another apart?" Nancy demanded.

Carmella dropped her eyes to the ground. Elsa felt completely at a loss for her words.

"Your father always said you girls were much more alike than you even knew," Nancy continued, lowering her voice the slightest bit. "He said that you'd probably never figure it out, that there was too much water under the bridge, but you should know that it was something he always prayed for regardless. He wanted you, girls, to come together, and dammit, I've done my best to be understanding, but the more you girls act like complete children, the more I want to treat you like them. God knows we've all had our heartaches the past few years. I know you Remington girls have had hardships up the wazoo. But for God's sake, why don't you try on a little empathy for one another for a change, huh? Stop making every last thing a competition. Otherwise, the cracks between you will follow through into this family. They will find ways to affect Mallory, Cole, Alexie and even Zachery, and I know you don't want that. I know your love is better than that. Both of you, just stop and think about that for a minute!"

Nancy rushed for the wine rack, grabbed another bottle, and then stomped out the door. Carmella clacked her way out the doorway as well but stepped leftward toward the driveway. In a moment, there was the jangling of her keys. Clearly, she had made up her mind to run away from the situation again. This was always her way.

Now, alone in the silence, Elsa replayed her own hurtful

words in her mind. How immature she had been to feed into such pettiness.

Why did she always revert to her teenage self when Carmella was around?

Why couldn't she overcome the past?

She drew her teeth over her lower lip as another memory flung through her.

Karen had been her ultimate enemy, and she still lingered many years after Neal had cut her from their lives for good.

# Chapter Sixteen

24 YEARS EARLIER

It was Elsa's twenty-first birthday. She was an Aries baby — although her younger sister, Carmella, frequently liked to say Elsa was nothing but a Taurus. *"You're so boring. All you do is stay home. You always want to know what will happen next. You're so predictable."* Carmella, a typical Scorpio, was always ready for an argument. It had always been this way, at least, since Colton's accident and their mother's death.

They hadn't seen eye to eye since.

But still, Elsa was firm in her belief in the beauty of family. She had a two-year-old son, Cole, whom she now balanced on her outer hip, even as her eight-month pregnant belly protruded dangerously out under her summer dress. Her husband, Aiden, drew open the door to her father's house and balanced the cake with his sturdy right hand. His eyes found hers as a smile inched across his face.

"Twenty-one years old. We'd better go out partying tonight, right, baby? Hit up all the clubs? You're finally legal!"

"Ha." Elsa rolled her eyes back as she sauntered, belly-first, into the house she had grown up in. "It's up to you to take me out when our little girl comes out of me. This summer, we're going dancing, mister. You promised."

"I did, didn't I?" Aiden dropped a kiss on her cheek as he led her deeper into the house.

"There they are." Karen, Elsa's stepmother of the previous year, stepped out of the kitchen. She wore a highly fashionable apron with little frills across the shoulders, and her dark black bob highlighted the sharp contours of her face. In the years since Elsa had met the woman, she'd hardly delivered a single smile.

And even now, it seemed, she forgot to say happy birthday. How marvelous.

"Carmella is helping me with the tortillas," Karen announced. "She just ran out to pick up more wine from that new little wine shop."

"Great." Elsa tried her darndest to feign a smile, but it still faltered. "Isn't she, um, only eighteen?"

Karen waved a hand flippantly. "I'm friends with the owner. She set aside the wine for Carmella to pick up. And in my mind, you know, I spent so much time in Europe, abroad. It's silly not to let Carmella have a few glasses of wine with the rest of us. She's eighteen, not eight. It's really just silly, the way this country handles some things like that."

Perhaps from anyone else, this might have seemed like logic. Elsa just bristled at everything Karen said, regardless. She longed to say something like, *Well, why don't you move back abroad and leave us all the hell alone?* But she kept those

118

thoughts to herself. She was a lady. She was her mother's kind and considerate soul.

Aiden took Cole from Elsa, stating he would change him in the other room. In truth, Elsa knew that Aiden felt strange in the company of Karen. He wanted to escape. "The woman is cold as ice," he'd said when he had first met her. "I don't know what your father sees in her. He's the warmest man on the planet."

It was true. The only answer Elsa had for this was that maybe, opposites attracted? It was difficult to say. Karen had begun work in acupuncture at the Katama Lodge and Wellness Spa. Neal had fallen for her beauty and her wit. She was the direct antithesis of Elsa's mother, Tina, who had passed away five years earlier.

When Neal had remarried, Elsa had been initially happy for him. After all, she felt that everyone deserved second chances. Everyone deserved happiness.

But this woman? What kind of joy could she possibly have brought into this house?

\* \* \*

An hour later, Elsa and Aiden sat on the back porch table across from Neal. Neal lifted his glass of wine toward Elsa and beamed. "I can't believe that my first child came into this world twenty-one years ago today. Where did the time go? And now, you're a mother yourself— almost twice over. Your own mother would be so proud of you, you know. She always knew that you would grow into such a beautiful, wonderful woman."

Elsa blinked back tears. "Thanks, Dad. That means a lot. I miss her so much."

"She's still here," Neal said softly. "Sometimes, when I'm out here alone at night, I feel like I can see her walking along the water. She always loved to run through the waves.

Remember that? You and Carmella and Colton all out there together. My perfect little family."

Neal grew wistful. Elsa's throat tightened so much that she found it difficult to breathe.

At that moment, Karen bolted through the screen door and arched an overly-plucked eyebrow. "Carmella and I are nearly finished with dinner. Is everyone ready for it?"

"Of course." Elsa put on her happiest, brightest voice. "Thank you so much."

Karen smirked as she dropped down to kiss Neal's cheek. Neal made no motion to return it. Instead, he turned his eyes back out toward the water as though still in the midst of picturing his deceased wife and son.

The homemade tortillas and taco fixings were remarkable. There was salmon, shrimp and crab and beef toppings, along with onion, salsa, guacamole and tiny sliced-up limes. Elsa tried to catch her little sister's eye to say thank you, but Carmella seemed to avoid her every try. Midway through dinner, Cole managed to smear a huge thing of refried beans across his cheek. Elsa chuckled and stood to take him into the kitchen to clean up.

"Baby, you don't have to do that," Aiden said midway through his taco.

"Don't worry. I'm full," Elsa said with a smile. "I'll be right back."

When she entered the kitchen, she found Carmella at the sink, filling up a glass of water. She turned, surprised to find Colton and Elsa there. It had been a long time since the two sisters had spent any time alone. Carmella stepped up and squeezed Cole's chubby baby arm.

"He's getting so big," Carmella said softly.

"And so am I." Elsa gestured toward her baby bump and winked.

Carmella lent Elsa a rare smile as Elsa placed Cole on the counter and reached for a paper towel.

"I can't believe how long it's been since I saw you," Elsa finally said. "The Lodge has been so busy lately, and juggling a toddler with the pregnancy has made me feel a bit strung out."

"No worries. I'm busy with senior year, anyway."

"How is that going?" Elsa felt that her own senior year at Edgartown High School was something like a million years ago — not three. How quickly the time had gone.

"Oh, fine. You know. Prom is next weekend. Whatever." Carmella's face told another story — one of excitement for this prominent event in a young woman's life.

"Do you have a date?"

Carmella dropped her eyelashes over her cheeks. "I do. But don't tell Dad."

"Tell me!" Elsa cried.

Carmella chuckled. "It's just this guy in my math class. He drives me insane. He confessed that he's liked me all of high school. I can't believe it's taken this long for him to finally tell me."

"Guys can be so shy when it comes to girls," Elsa returned. "But it's complicated, isn't it? Since you're headed to college next year? I guess you can have a nice little summer romance beforehand."

Carmella's face shifted the slightest bit. She turned back toward the dishwasher and crossed her arms over her chest. "Actually, I decided not to go to college next year."

Elsa's heart pounded strangely. "What do you mean?"

"It's not like you went to college."

"I was pregnant pretty immediately and had other things on my mind. But you know that I've been taking night classes for the past year, right?" Elsa bristled at Carmella's sudden attitude. "Getting an education is so important, Carmella. Mom would have wanted it for you."

Carmella's eyes darkened at the mention of their mother. "Mom didn't care about what was best for me. You know that."

A lump formed in Elsa's throat. Here it was again— Carmella's endless story about how their mother had never forgiven Carmella for what had happened to Colton.

Of course, what had happened to Colton wouldn't have happened without Carmella there.

That was true.

But nobody pointed it out any longer. Nobody demanded any kind of apology or sacrifice.

"Mom loved you, Carm," Elsa said softly. "There's no way around that."

"Sure. Because she had to," Carmella insisted. She stabbed her finger on the counter formidably, then added, "Karen showed me this program in the southwest. I can learn to do acupuncture there. It's like a three-month thing, and you travel around and learn from all these instructors. I think it's perfect for me."

Elsa stiffened. "You've never spoken about this before— never in your life."

Carmella shrugged. "I mean, I think what Karen does is insanely cool. It's like drugs, but without all the bad side effects. She really opens people's minds. I could do that."

"I mean, nothing says you shouldn't do that eventually. I just think you should follow your original plan of going to school," Elsa returned.

Shadows formed beneath Carmella's eyes. "I don't know why you're pretending to be Mom right now because you're not even remotely close to her."

Elsa heaved a sigh. "I've just talked to you about what you want for the past three or four years. I thought we had a pretty clear strategy."

"Karen says that you want to live out your fantasies through me. She says that because you didn't get to go to school, because you got knocked up, you want to put all this pressure on me. Well, I'm sick of it." Carmella lifted her chin angrily.

Elsa gave all her strength not to roll her eyes as far back into her skull as she could. Of course, yet again, Karen had attempted to draw a huge line between the two sisters. Throughout her marriage to Neal, she'd drawn Carmella closer and closer and shoved Elsa further and further away. Neal had even admitted that he had sensed it once, although he'd struggled to speak ill of his new wife.

It was natural that he didn't want to admit the fact that he'd chosen so poorly.

"Can't we just talk about this?" Elsa asked as she slid the paper towel over her son's cheek. He buzzed his lips up at her playfully. He hadn't any idea her and her sister's relationship was in the midst of a strange, dying gasp.

"There's nothing to talk about. I've made up my mind," Carmella returned. "And I'm sure Dad will give me the money to go once I tell him."

"Great. It sounds like you have a perfect, new strategy for your life. Be an acupuncturist, like Karen before you." Elsa struggled to hold back her sarcasm. "I'm sure Mom would be so proud."

"Oh, don't you dare! I don't care what Mom thinks," Carmella blurted. "It's a waste of time living in the past. You're going to pop out another baby soon and I'm going to go find myself out west. Elsa, we're different, so different that there's basically no use in fighting about this. Karen thinks that the sooner we separate ourselves from one another, the sooner we can heal."

Anger flashed across Elsa's face. "What did you just say?"

Carmella shrugged flippantly. "You heard me."

Elsa let out a strange laugh. "You can't let that woman get between us."

"That woman? That woman happens to be my mother,"

Carmella sneered at her sister.

"Oh, here we go..." Elsa rolled her eyes back, then. "She's been around like five seconds, and you're putting all your eggs in that basket —"

"I'm pretty sure Dad married her. Pretty sure we were both there for that legally binding ceremony," Carmella returned.

Elsa finished up Cole's cheek and lifted him back into her. "I don't want to fight with you on my birthday," she snapped. "But just so you know, I'm going to talk to Dad about your future, and he's going to hear about Karen's little attempt to break up our family. Is that clear?"

"Now, who sounds like my mother?" Carmella blurted.

Several days later, Elsa drummed up the courage to head into her father's office to discuss what Carmella had told her about Karen, along with Carmella's less-than-stellar plans for her future. When she stepped into her father's office, Neal had his face in his hands and his shoulders hunched. Sunshine streamed in through the window just behind the desk so that he was bathed in light. But he looked like a portrait of a defeated man.

"Dad?"

When Neal lifted his eyes toward Elsa's, Elsa's heart dropped. Strangely, the baby then smacked her foot against the base of her belly, as though she'd sensed the shift in mood, too.

"Hey, honey," Neal said. "Why don't you sit down?"

Elsa did. It wasn't like she could stand for long, given her current state, anyway.

"I wanted to talk to you about Karen," Elsa finally whispered.

And then, the pregnancy hormones fought against her, and she promptly burst into tears as she explained herself. "I just don't know about this woman, Daddy. I don't understand why you married her. And now, she's telling Carmella that I don't have her best interests at heart and that I don't love her. Daddy, I do love her. She's my sister for God's sake, but you know how complicated it is to love Carmella, sometimes. You know!"

When Elsa lifted her head once more, she found her father's face filled with its own round of tears. He reached for a handkerchief and flung it to the side to collect them, then pushed the handkerchief back in his pocket.

"I regret almost everything right now, Elsa. Almost everything." His eyes finally found hers; they were soft and earnest. "But I don't know what to do about it."

Elsa's throat tightened. She tried to speak, yet she failed.

"I will tell Karen it's over soon," he finally whispered. "But Carmella will be heartbroken. The girl loves Karen more than I can really understand. I hear them whispering and laughing together deep into the night. I have no idea what they're talking about, and I can't help but think that Karen has poisoned Carmella far more than even you or I can sense. Still, I suppose it's better to cut it off while we still can. Hopefully, her infectious behavior won't spread too far."

Elsa nodded. She reached across the desk and gripped her father's hand. To the side, she spotted a framed photograph of Neal and Karen on their wedding day a couple of years prior. In other times, that same frame had held a photograph of her mother and Neal on their wedding day — twenty-two years before.

Apparently, Karen had decided to switch the photos.

It made Elsa's heart burn with rage.

"She was never a Remington. Not really," Elsa blurted out as she lifted her chin. "I know we can recover from this, Daddy. We've fought through everything else."

"I sure hope you're right," he whispered, as his dark blue eyes stirred with longing and sorrow.

# Chapter Seventeen

M allory yanked little Zachery's polka-dotted swim trunks high up so that they grazed past his belly button and made him look like Steve Urkel.

"He just needs a pair of suspenders, and he's all set for age eighty," Alyssa teased as she patted his stomach gently.

Mallory cackled and tossed her head back. Mallory, Maggie, and Alyssa sat in gorgeous bikinis, with their full tresses billowing out in the sea breeze. They looked like cousins, completely and totally instead of the step-cousins they actually were. Throughout the previous days of Maggie and Alyssa's stay, the three of them had latched on to one another remarkably, sharing secrets in Maggie and Alyssa's guest bedroom and taking little Zachery around with them every-where. He had already been featured prominently in Maggie's social media channels, and as Maggie was something of a Manhattan socialite, a number of incredibly famous Manhat-tan-ites had written her to exclaim, "What a beautiful baby! Who is that little thing?" Maggie had just written back, "The most adorable baby on Martha's Vineyard — my first cousin, once removed."

Elsa sat back on her own towel alongside Janine and Nancy. Nancy lifted her chin toward the blue sky above, and as Elsa viewed the full breadth of this woman's beauty, an airplane trickled across the reflection of her sunglasses.

"Every day is so perfect here," Janine breathed as she stretched her shoulders back. "And I'm so glad we took today off. I was getting burned out. I hate to admit it."

"It's only natural. We give so much to the women at the Lodge. We have to keep something back for ourselves, too," Nancy said.

Elsa remained silent. Since her spat with Carmella several nights before, she had been overwhelmed with pain and anger toward herself. She wasn't used to Nancy pointing out her flaws; the woman had only ever demonstrated kindness and compassion toward her. Nancy more or less knew the entire story of Carmella and Elsa and still, she had found reason to demand they take a good, hard look at themselves and find a way to repair the cracks between them. What she had said continued to echo through Elsa's mind: that if they weren't strong enough to fight their hatred toward one another, the pain of it all would transfer down to the future generations in the family. She supposed Nancy knew this better than most, as so much of her own pain had fallen onto Janine's shoulders. It would take years to mend what had begun so long before.

Nancy stood from her towel and stretched her arms toward the sky. Her maroon one-piece suit fit her trim frame beautifully. Elsa had helped her pick it out at a little boutique downtown during happier times, a few weeks before even Janine had arrived on the island. "I suppose it'll be just us on the beach this summer," Nancy had told Elsa at the time. "But I dare say, I'll still look good out there."

How wrong Nancy had been. They were surrounded with light and with love. Elsa tried to demand her heart to soak in every moment.

Nancy took Baby Zachery in her arms and bobbed him playfully. She then sauntered down toward the waves and dipped herself in until the water swirled up around her knees. All the while, Zachery squealed joyously and gazed up at his step-grandmother with all the love in the world.

"It's so cute how much that little boy loves Mom," Janine commented. "Although I have to admit. I never imagined Nancy Grimson becoming the kind of woman who actually loved a life of domesticity. Look at her! She looks like a natural. It's true that anyone can learn anything. We are such adaptable creatures."

Mallory, Maggie, and Alyssa sprung up from their towels and headed over to the little beach-side cafe for wine slushies. This left Elsa and Janine alone. The pressing weight of the moment gave Elsa pause. There was somehow so much pressure; after all, she and Janine hardly spent any time together alone, and it wasn't like Elsa didn't stir with resentment toward her.

Janine placed her hand on her own knee and stretched her fingers out wide. It seemed that she didn't know what to say to Elsa, either. Out in the waves, Nancy twirled in circles, making Zachery screech.

"Do you mind if I ask you something, Elsa?"

Janine's words yanked Elsa from her reverie. She blinked, then nodded, genuinely surprised. Maybe this was how they would find common ground. Maybe they just had to leap for it.

"All my life, I wanted a sister. Maggie and Alyssa have this incredible relationship. Sometimes, it's like they don't have to speak at all to be understood. Growing up, I had — well, Maxine. Maxine Aubert was my very best friend and my confidant. I guess you know what happened there."

Elsa's heart thudded with sorrow. "I can't even imagine what that must have been like."

It was true. Although loss and death had followed her around for decades, no one in Elsa's life had ever wronged her. Nobody had ever double-crossed her. She just had bad luck. But luck had nothing to do with someone you loved digging a knife in your back. That was evil, pure and simple.

Janine shrugged. "It will probably take me years and years of therapy and prayer and conversation to fully get over the hurt Maxine caused. I've been given a tremendous gift, in that my mother opened up her arms to me. I really couldn't have asked for anything more. She's been my saving grace.

"But beyond that, since I arrived on the island, I've noticed that you and Carmella aren't exactly the closest of sisters. In fact, if I hadn't first seen Carmella at the house, I would have thought you two were more like strangers. Or even enemies."

Elsa's cheeks grew hot with the sudden influx of Janine's words. She turned her eyes toward the beach, where she realized she'd dug through to the base of the cold, wet sand below with her pinky finger. She'd been so anxious; she hadn't even noticed.

"It's none of my business to ask, maybe, but what happened between the two of you?" Janine finally breathed.

Elsa buzzed her lips and continued to blink down at the sand. In all her years, she'd never had to fully explain the story of herself and Carmella. It had just been standard island gossip that the Remington sisters didn't see eye to eye and never got along. They'd managed to work alongside one another for a number of years since Carmella had returned from her stint out west with her acupuncture certification, but they had done so with minimal conversation and communion.

"Carmella and I never really saw eye to eye, I guess," Elsa said.

"That sounds like a caged response." Janine's voice lilted the slightest bit.

Elsa laughed. "Because it is, I guess. Just something to say."

"You really can tell me if you want to," Janine assured her. "It's not like I have anyone to tell."

Elsa sucked in her cheeks. Down below, Zachery let out another squeal.

"Your mother hasn't spoken to you about it very much?"

Janine shook her head. "Just in passing. Just said basically the same as you and also mentioned that you know, Neal hated the fact that you two couldn't get along."

"Dad and I were really close," Elsa offered. Again, the cracks in her heart showed on the surface as tears sprung to her eyes. "Carmella and Dad fought quite a bit, same as me and Carm. But Dad loved her to pieces. He always wanted what was best for her. Sometimes, that meant crossing the line — like when he tried to buy her an apartment, or when he tried to set her up with a guy he'd met in Oak Bluffs, or when he tried to get her to sign up to therapy."

"She didn't want to go, I take it?"

Elsa eased a strand of hair behind her ear. "We were both resistant to it for different reasons. I just wanted to be strong all the time, for everyone. I guess I have a chip on my shoulder about it, although I've kind of lost that strength recently. I've felt myself waning. Like the light has gone out of my eyes."

"That light is still there," Janine murmured. "I promise you that."

Elsa glanced up to find Janine's warm, welcoming eyes.

"Our father married a woman when I was nineteen. A woman named Karen," Elsa continued. "Carmella was sixteen and in the height of her teenage angst phase, you know? You can imagine Carmella in teenage angst."

"Sometimes, it seems like she hasn't grown out of it," Janine said lightly.

"True." Elsa realized a tear had rolled down her cheek as she spoke, and she swiped it away hurriedly. "Anyway, I was immediately wary of Karen and her agenda. She was uptight and volatile and I swear, I never saw her smile a genuine smile. I think Dad was lonely, and she came along hunting for his money. She spoke sweetly to him, and she doted on Carmella. Carmella was the only one in the house, and I think she wanted to sway her toward Karen's side as some kind of weapon against my father. Carmella was so broken back then. So broken! And Karen thought if this young girl needs me, maybe Neal will keep me around longer. But ultimately, Karen built a wall between Carmella and me. Our already strained relationship became impossible. And then... I told Dad what was happening. I told him how Karen was behaving and how she was digging her heels into Carmella because I was really worried. But I was also spiteful and angry. Anyway, after that, Dad almost immediately kicked Karen out of the house, and Carmella blamed me for everything."

"Gosh. That sounds so awful and complicated," Janine whispered.

"It really was," Elsa returned. "On top of it all, Mallory had just been born as this all happened, and I had my hands full with Cole. I felt like I couldn't really be there for Carmella anyway, to repair things the way I knew I needed to. By the time she got back from the southwest, she seemed like an entirely different woman — nobody I had ever met before. Only once did she say, 'You know, Karen was the only person who ever loved me for me.' But after that, she dropped it for years. I could just feel her anger through her eyes, you know. She had never let go of the resentment and anger."

"I've noticed that her eyes almost hold some kind of darkness behind them, like a storm of pain. She looks so conflicted at times," Janine affirmed. "You can't really place what she's thinking at any one time."

"She's always been that way," Elsa said softly.

"Mom! We got you this." Mallory dropped down to the towel to deliver a wine slushie.

Elsa gripped the chilly plastic cup and thanked Mallory. She could still feel the heaviness of Janine's gaze as she studied her and dove through the events of the previous few years. When Mallory glanced up to begin another conversation with the arriving Maggie and Alyssa, Janine wrapped her hand around Elsa's elbow and said, "Just one more thing."

Elsa's heart felt squeezed. They'd walked so far down memory lane that she could no longer see where they'd begun. "What is it?"

"I just think Carmella might be one of the loneliest people I've met in my life," Janine said. "If you can find it within you to try to forgive her for everything — if you can find it within you to attempt to mend it, well." She then flipped her hair behind her shoulders and let out a beautiful laugh, a laugh more like a song than anything else.

"But listen to me— giving you all this unsolicited advice. You're not one of my patients. You're my sister, too. And if you need anything, anything at all, then I'm here for you. I know it's maybe too early to say this, but I love you. My mother loves you. And we have a whole lot to be grateful for. It's just, when I see Carmella, I wonder if everything always has to be that way. You know?"

Nancy cast a shadow as she approached from the rushing waves. Zachery's tired eyes seemed to have sunk deeper into his chunky face. He bobbed an arm and let out a small cry as Mallory hopped up and wrapped her arms around him and held him off to the left of her torso. Deep in the distance, a twin set of sailboats chased one another in frantic circles. Somehow, the ocean felt immense from their stance on the beach as it belled out and became unfathomably deep, filled with unknowable secrets and long-lost histories.

Elsa had always known this about the ocean. Yet she had also felt that her own soul was similar: that the hugeness of her love for her family was akin to the ocean. She simply couldn't see the bottom. Carmella, perhaps, was her ocean's hurricane.

# Chapter Eighteen

Elsa felt just like those younger women who were at the bar the other day: eager to please and the tiniest bit frantic as she leaned closer to the rearview mirror and drew a delicate black line from one corner of her eye to the other. She had a meeting at the Susan Sheridan law office in fifteen minutes, and for reasons she couldn't fully comprehend, she had decided to splash on the tiniest amount of perfume and purchase a new sharp, black eyeliner pencil from CVS en route. Probably, those young women would have told her she was dismal at putting on eyeliner. They probably would have been right.

Ah, but she didn't look so bad. She puffed out her cheeks and assessed her work, then blinked down at the outfit she'd chosen for the meeting. It was a button-down pink blouse with the sweetest and tenderest of buttons, round and vintage, along with a pair of dark jeans, which Mallory had spotted as Elsa had hustled through the living room, hunting for her keys. "They make your butt look amazing, Mom," Mallory had said. "Shush, you," Elsa had returned, as her cheeks had flashed what had probably been the brightest shade of crimson.

Elsa hadn't told Mallory where she was off to. Still, nobody knew about the lawsuit. Aiden's name was safe, as was how handsome her lawyer was. Sometimes, even the slightest attraction was secret from herself, just a fantasy somewhere in the back of her mind. It had no value in the real world at all.

Minutes later, Elsa found herself again in the foyer of the Sheridan law office. She clasped her hands over her lap as Amanda Harris informed her Bruce would be available shortly. Amanda then returned to her notepad and furrowed her brow. At that moment, a young, handsome man in his mid-twenties burst into the office. Amanda blinked up as a wide smile crested her lips. The man held a plate of brownies and croissants in his outstretched hand.

"You didn't!" Amanda cried.

"Oh, but I did."

"I told you I couldn't eat all those sweets during the day anymore."

"And I told you, Miss Harris, that you deserve all the sweetness in the world." The man placed the platter before Amanda, as Amanda's eyes remained latched to his.

"Sam…" Even as she protested, Elsa could sense the love that emanated from her eyes.

Elsa wondered who this young man was. She wondered what was in store for these young people.

But more than that, as she witnessed their beautiful flirtation, she was cast back to her own memories — ones between her and Aiden and their courtship. That had been the time for joy, for light, for hope.

And this — this time of silly eyeliner and butterflies in her stomach? Wasn't it foolish of her?

Oh, but then, Bruce drew open the door of his office. He stood in the doorway and beamed out across the space between them. When his eyes found hers, Elsa was reminded of the afternoon when he'd discovered her cast back on the trail, her head screaming with pain. She had read somewhere that women always latched to people emotionally when they'd saved them. She thought maybe it was a hormonal thing.

But she didn't care. Not then.

"Mrs. Steel. Hello," Bruce greeted her.

Elsa's heart sank the slightest bit. Perhaps he wanted to maintain some sense of professionalism in front of Amanda and her handsome friend? Or maybe, he thought nothing of her at all.

"Mr. Holland," she replied with a wide smile. "Good to see you."

Elsa followed Bruce into his office and sat in the seat across from his. Aiden's box of files remained in the corner of the office, on top of a large wardrobe. Elsa was fully aware of the time and commitment it must have taken Bruce to analyze each of the pages within.

As Bruce sat, Elsa found her voice.

"Thank you again for the other day."

Bruce bowed his head as a playful smile snuck across his face. "It was my pleasure. It's not every day that a man is allowed to literally save someone."

Elsa felt the sudden desire to tease him. "Guess it boosted your ego?"

"Oh yes. Thank you for that."

Bruce held her gaze for a long moment and then dropped it down to the manila folder before him. "I've gone through a number of Aiden's client cases so far."

"Including the one with Carlson Montague?"

Bruce clucked his tongue. "There are a number of files missing when it comes to that case. It's peculiar, as Aiden was really organized when it came to his business."

Elsa's heart pounded louder. "Doesn't that mean there's something really odd going on?"

"It's difficult to prove any of that, unfortunately," Bruce said. His smile faltered even more.

"But you must be able to speak with this Carlson guy or his lawyer? I mean, if you saw him, you'd know that there's something really strange about him. He's spreading misinformation. And he — well..."

Elsa furrowed her brow at the memory of those girls from the other night at the bar. Bruce leaned tighter across the desk. With him came the pleasant rush of his cologne.

"What is it? Anything you can give me might be of help, Elsa. Really. I know you've been a part of this community for a long time. If you can think of anything at all, it will help."

"Well, I met my son at one of the local bars that these men frequent the other night." Elsa's heart now threatened to bang out of her rib cage. She felt reckless. "Because I wanted to just see what these men were like, you know when their tongues were looser and maybe not wary of being watched."

Bruce arched a thick eyebrow. "I see. You wanted to spy on them."

"Something like that. But I was nervous and I wasn't sure if they would recognize me. But then I noticed that they had these three women with them— very young women in their early twenties."

"Not so strange for rich men in the sailing community, right? They like their arm candy."

"No. I guess not." Elsa felt a wave of shame come over her, but she pushed herself forward. "I followed the girls into the bathroom."

"Wow. You really have nerves of steel."

"No. I don't know. I was just really curious and you know how girls are in the bathroom."

"Not really," Bruce said with a laugh. "You hear stories."

"Well, things are a little more chummy, let's put it that way. And suddenly, the girls were telling me that they work as... what was that word? Escorts?"

Bruce raised his eyebrows still higher. "Still, not so surprising for this world, right?"

"No. I guess not. But they said that these guys bring them everywhere, that they pay for everything, including their apartment in the city and their trips abroad and well everything. It's more like —"

"Sugar daddies," Bruce said finally. "I've heard about this, too. I think it means there's a definite emotional element at play, which means that maybe these guys are more open about their personal lives."

"Exactly." Elsa snapped as she swept toward the front of her chair with excitement. "And one of the girls — the red-haired one, although I guess that means nothing to you."

"Not to me. I'm no police officer," Bruce returned.

"Right. But she mentioned stuff about offshore accounts and illegal dealings. And she really insinuated that these men didn't want anything from them other than companionship and nothing more. I didn't have the heart to tell them that men like this always expected more."

"They certainly find ways to move on," Bruce agreed. He then reached for his pen and clacked the end of it with a wayward thumb, lost in thought. "This is interesting. I mean, but it doesn't really mean anything, does it?"

Elsa buzzed her lips. "I don't know. Maybe? I mean, it shows this Carlson guy is a bad guy. Why does he have offshore accounts or illegal dealings?"

"Sure. But there are loads of shady guys out there. It doesn't mean your husband didn't wrong him in some way."

There was silence between them. Bruce's eyes fell to the pad of paper on the desk. After a long pause, he added, "I didn't mean that. I'm sorry, but I have to speculate at best."

"It's okay. I understand," Elsa said hurriedly. "I know you didn't."

After a long pause, Bruce buzzed his lips and ran his fingers through his thick hair. "I want to go for a walk. Would you be interested in a walk? It's a beautiful day, and I've spent almost all of it locked between these four walls."

\* \* \*

A few minutes later, Elsa and Bruce walked along the waterway near the Oak Bluffs harbor. In the distance, a ferry swept forth, straight from Woods Hole in Falmouth, and within, another rampant collection of tourists approached. Elsa could feel the excitement beaming from the tip-top of the ferry like a cloud. How strange the concept of "vacation" was. She'd hardly taken one a day in her life. She supposed that's what it meant to grow up in paradise — if paradise was really what this was.

Elsa placed her hands over the wooden railing that trailed up toward the western part of the island, over where the Sunrise Cove Inn swelled, overlooking the ocean. Her lump in her throat seemed bigger than ever at that moment.

"Maybe you could still interview those girls. See what they say?" Elsa finally asked.

Bruce nodded. He clutched the railing, too. Elsa wondered what he thought, or why he'd asked her outside, or what he really thought of Aiden, especially after perusing all of his paperwork. Did Bruce maybe think that Aiden had done what Carlson Montague had said? Was it possible that Aiden had done all that?

It chilled her to the bone to actually ask that question.

She'd known Aiden to his core. She had known how he liked to sleep and how much milk to put in his coffee and which movie always made him cry (*Good Will Hunting*, every single time). She'd loved him to pieces, even the messy parts of him and with him gone, she was a hollowed-out mess.

"What was your wife like?" Elsa asked it so tentatively that it even came as a surprise to herself.

Bruce clutched the wooden rail still harder, although his energy remained the same: sure, calm. Something to lean on.

"She was much funnier than me," he finally said. "When she entered a room, she knew exactly what to say to make everyone burst into laughter. Sometimes, she brought me to tears with her jokes. I realized, when I stayed on at the house we'd lived in together, I hadn't laughed in weeks— maybe months. It tore me apart, knowing that, but it's also part of the reason I came back here. My brother and sister both live here on the island, and they're funny but not as funny as she was. They make me fall apart sometimes with laughter. It's good for the soul, that's for sure. It's true what they say about that."

Elsa feigned confusion and furrowed her brow. "What do you mean? Who says what about what?"

Bruce spread out his large palms and blinked at her. "You know— about laughter. And medicine."

Elsa shook her head doubtfully. "Laughter? And medicine?"

Bruce looked aghast. "You seriously haven't heard that?"

Elsa winced. "Ooo no. Bruce Holland doesn't understand sarcasm. That's a minus two on the old point system."

Suddenly, Bruce's face grew electric. He tossed his head back as laughter rolled from his lips. He smacked his hand on the railing so hard that it shook.

"You really got me. Jeez. I can't believe it."

Elsa joined him in laughter, and her stomach spasmed. "It wasn't even that funny of a joke!"

"I know. I know. But I really needed it," Bruce told her warmly as the last of his laughter died out. "Thank you for it, really."

Elsa dug her elbow into his bicep playfully. "I'll try to come up with a few more jokes for you, but only if you do the same for me?"

"That's a deal," he told her. "I'm going to hold you to that one."

# Chapter Nineteen

Bruce and Elsa returned back to Elsa's vehicle about a half hour later. Elsa lifted her eyes to Bruce's as she began to thank him for the conversation and his kindness. But at that moment, Bruce lifted his phone to find a message.

"One second." He tapped through his phone, then paused for a long time as he blinked down at it.

From Elsa's vantage point, all she could see was a dark screen. Annoyance ballooned in her stomach. Why hadn't he waited another few minutes to check on this after she had left?

But at that moment, everything changed. His eyes found hers again as he turned the phone screen toward her. Elsa's heart dropped into her stomach, and a low moan crept out of her throat. Nothing about this was right. Nothing about this was fair.

Bruce had brought up a newspaper article. And the headline read:

**LOCAL STOCKBROKER AIDEN STEEL**

## PURPORTEDLY MISHANDLED FUNDS AND STOLE FROM TRUSTING CLIENTS

Beneath the headline, the idiot journalist had actually put a photo of Aiden, one that had been featured on his website for all to see. Elsa hadn't bothered to even think about taking the website down. Doing that would have meant yet again that he was really gone. Now, she regretted it.

"No." Elsa gripped the phone still harder and blinked up at Bruce. Her knees clacked together. "No. Why did they write this? I don't understand. There's no proof. You told me yourself that there's no proof."

Bruce's nostrils flared. "That's why they wrote 'purportedly.' There's nothing to go on. They're just interviewing this Carlson guy and whoever else wants their fifteen minutes of fame. Dammit." He took his phone back and ran his free fingers through his hair in the act of frustration.

Awkwardness permeated the air between them. Their beautiful walk had been squashed. Elsa reached for her keys but immediately dropped them on the ground as her hands shook horribly.

"I want to drive you home," Bruce said. His voice was firm, something to cling to as the world shattered around her.

"That's silly. You don't have to do that." Even as she spoke, she felt herself falling away from present consciousness. Shadows formed on the outside of her vision, so she steadied herself against the car as sweat pooled across her neck.

"Please. I want to. I'll even drive your car."

Elsa waded to the passenger seat. Her arms spasmed as she reached for the seat belt and strung it over her lap. Bruce turned on the engine and muttered to himself, words Elsa could hardly make out.

"What was that?"

"Nothing. I just want to call the newspaper. I can't believe they would put out such a damaging article." He grumbled again, then added, "Maybe this Carlson guy has a say in what's published. It's happened before. He might be a sponsor or —"

Bruce continued to mutter as they eased away from Oak Bluffs and swirled along the backroads all the way south. Elsa felt a sense of dread as they grew closer. She had attempted for the past few weeks to hide all this from her children, from her friends, from her family. Now, their ocean of lies was splayed out for all to see.

Bruce parked Elsa's car in the driveway and turned to look at her. Elsa might have made a joke about how he was too big for her car. His knees threatened to bang against the steering wheel, even though he'd adjusted it all the way up. He was a giant but such a tender, kind, and upstanding giant.

"Do you want me to come in with you? I can explain everything we know so far to your family," Bruce offered.

Elsa shook her head. "No. I need to face this alone, I think."

"You're not alone in this, Elsa. You never have been." Bruce set his jaw. After a moment, he pressed open the car door and stepped out. He informed her he would walk the rest of the way to his place, seeing it wasn't far and that he needed to clear his head.

Just then, the sadness made her body feel overwhelmed with exhaustion. She felt like a slug. She watched him from the front porch as he disappeared behind the line of trees, now completely out of view. For the first time, she tried to picture what his bachelor pad might look like. What a strange thing it might have been to live alone after so much time with a spouse. She hoped he wasn't lonely. But loneliness was a necessary part of life, wasn't it? Even Elsa was lonely sometimes, even when around her nearest and dearest.

The house seemed drafty and quiet. Elsa stepped through and discovered Nancy and Janine on the back porch. They stood around Mallory, who had her face in her hands. Her shoulders shook. Alongside her in his baby seat, Zachery whacked a plastic spoon around playfully.

The screen door creaked open. Mallory lifted her eyes to her mother's, and her chin quivered.

"Did you know about this?" Mallory breathed.

Elsa paused for a long time. There was so much to say, and still, so much she didn't know.

"He didn't do anything wrong," Elsa finally said.

"How can you know that?" Mallory whispered.

"Because I knew your father for twenty-seven years. He was the most honest man I've ever known. He wouldn't have done this. He wouldn't have put us in a position like this after his death. I would bet my life on it."

Nancy fell back into one of the porch chairs and dotted a handkerchief across her forehead. Janine sipped her wine and blinked at the floor.

After a long pause, Nancy cleared her throat.

"You're right, Elsa. I really don't believe it, either. And these rich men who come to the island for sailing season — they can really be problematic. No way to know what these guys' motives are."

Elsa nodded, even as her eyes welled with tears. Mallory remained speechless. Just then, Elsa's phone began to vibrate in her purse. She lifted it to find Cole's name. Soon, she knew, Alexie would also be calling from New York City. The cat was out of the bag.

"I have a lawyer handling this, Mal," Elsa said as she lifted her phone to her ear. "We will clear your father's name. Mark my words, and then I'll sue this damn buffoon for defamation of character. Do you understand me?"

Cole, of course, already knew bits and pieces of his father's situation. But his silence on the other end of the line as Elsa explained what they knew so far was dark and menacing.

"Don't do anything rash, Cole," Elsa finally said. She half-imagined him ducking down to the docks and punching one of those guys in the face. "It isn't worth it. I don't want anyone to get in even more trouble."

Cole cleared his throat. There was the sound of whipping wind around his phone. Probably, he already stood out on one of those docks, nearest to his sailboat. She could picture him gazing out at the horizon line, sullen, volatile and angry. She wished she could take his pain away, all of their pain away.

"You really think we can trust him?" Cole finally asked.

Elsa's heart shattered. "Of course, we can trust him."

"I'm just starting to forget, Mom. What he was really like."

This was the worst possible thing for Cole to ever say. Elsa's eyes closed at the thought — that one day, even her memories of Aiden would be stretched thin. Maybe she wouldn't fully remember his face. Maybe she would have to watch old videos in order to remember his voice.

"He's still here with us, Cole. He's watching over us." Even as Elsa said it, she wasn't so sure. She was beginning to lose her grip on reality. Her throat tightened when she heard Cole weep through the other end of the line. It broke her heart in two.

Now that Cole was twenty-six years old, it was strange to hear him cry. Elsa begged him to come over, so they could be together as a family. But Cole said he couldn't. "I have to deal with this alone," he told her.

"I don't think anyone should be alone in this," Elsa told him. "Please. I love you. I want you here."

In the end, Cole gave in and did go back to Nancy's house. He sat sullenly on the back porch and sipped a beer. Throughout the stunted conversation, he crossed his arms over his chest and looked out across the water. Nancy continued to try to get everyone to eat, but everyone just refused. Even Janine sat with her shoulders hunched, acting gloomy. Both her girls had returned to the city, and there was sadness that shadowed her face.

Everyone at the table mourned a loss.

The following morning, Elsa drove out to the cemetery where they had buried Aiden's body beneath six feet of dirt. She and Mallory had planted tulips along the stone in the spring, and the flowers were boisterous and bright against the severe gray of the tombstone. Elsa fell onto the grass in front of it and traced his name in the rock with her finger.

"Tell me you didn't do this, Aiden. Tell me you didn't leave us with such a big mess."

Elsa wasn't sure what she expected. A hawk rushed overhead and cawed out. The sound was ominous, horrific; she decided it couldn't be any sign from Aiden. In some ways, she felt him less here at his grave than she did in other places on the island. After all, they had no memories at the cemetery together. Normally, she had visited her mother and brother's graves alone or with her father.

Notably, Carmella had never come with them. Not since her teenage years. And even then, Karen had gotten her out of those trips.

"I feel pretty alone without you here, Aiden," Elsa whispered. "You left me with all these clues that I can't make sense of, and a bunch of very rich, angry men who want to drag your name through the mud and then some. It kills me to think that so many islanders think poorly of you now. People love gossip. People love secrets. And these naysayers played into that perfectly."

Elsa buzzed her lips and lifted her chin toward the sky. Clouds lifted beautifully through the blue and they puffed around like cotton candy. She wanted to curse the gorgeous day; she longed for rain and turmoil, sharp wind instead— anything to match her mood.

"You always said God gives us just exactly what we can handle," Elsa breathed to the tombstone. "But I haven't been able to handle any of this and not very well. And I'm getting so tired, Aiden. I'm so, so tired."

As Elsa drove back to the Katama Lodge to get in a few hours of work, Bruce called her.

"I managed to track down a couple of those women you told me about," he said. "The ones who hang with these men. Two blond girls."

"Yes. There was one redhead and two blondes."

"Well, anyway. They're pretty hush-hush about anything to do with these guys. They mentioned trips to Paris and private planes and tickets to baseball games and all that, but they either don't know what Carlson Montague is up to, or they've made sure to wade their way around it."

Elsa buzzed her lips. "The red-haired one was the one who seemed to know the most. Maybe you could interview her?"

"I wasn't able to track her down. I asked the other girls about her, but they just shrugged and made up some excuse. I don't know where to go from here, really. It isn't a dead-end exactly, but..."

"I get it," Elsa said. "Thank you for trying."

"This isn't over, Elsa."

Elsa tried to believe in his words. Still, the heaviness of it all made her despondent. She thanked him again and then hung up the phone. Back in her office, she attempted to throw herself into her duties for the day; but sometimes, the anxiety of it all swept through her like the wind. She gazed out the window and demanded herself to breathe: in, out. In, out.

The only way forward was through. She had to believe that.

# Chapter Twenty

T he next few days dripped past. Elsa staggered through every hour. She caught herself staring out windows, blinking into space — her mind heavy with fears and panic. All the while, Bruce checked in with her without much news. It seemed they had run up against a brick wall. Islanders, too, had begun to look at Elsa with even more pity than they had previously. News of Aiden's "failings" had spread like wildfire. Now, Elsa had not only lost her husband and her father in a single year but was also the woman who had been left with a mess the size of Neptune.

"Tell me we won't have to pay this bastard all this money," Elsa breathed into the phone.

Bruce was quiet for a long time. He cleared his throat and then said, "I'm really going to do everything I can to make sure that doesn't happen."

"But you can't promise."

"I can only promise I'll be with you through this till the end."

Elsa dropped her head back after Bruce hung up. She

placed her phone on her chest and listened to her heart's subtle but ever-growing sound as it slammed around in her rib cage. Years ago, Aiden had placed his head on her heart as they'd lie together in bed. *"I love to listen to how alive you are,"* he'd said. The moment had always stuck with her — especially in the months since his own heart had stopped.

Elsa hung up the phone and lifted her fingers to her keyboard. Several emails demanded her attention. She struggled with spelling and grammar as though all of her intelligence had dripped out of her ears. She blinked out toward the window and thought for the first time in a long time that she might like to leave the island and go somewhere else— where nobody knew her or Aiden's name. There, she could live in the silence of herself, safe with her memories.

But to live in your memories was not living at all, and she knew that. In the wake of her brother's death and then her mother's death, she had forced herself forward. She had fallen in love and she'd gotten pregnant and then she had gotten married. Events had flung themselves forth and she'd loved every minute of that "carpe diem" mentality.

There was a knock on the door. Elsa glanced at her computer's calendar. No meetings were scheduled for another two hours.

"Come in?"

The door cracked the slightest bit. A tennis shoe opened it wider. Elsa furrowed her brow at the flash of dark curls and the large, ominous eyes. Carmella stood before her, and she did not smile.

Carmella hadn't exactly been high on Elsa's "see today" list. She'd avoided her since their argument in the kitchen when Nancy had scolded them. Janine's words regarding Carmella had rolled around the back of Elsa's mind, for sure, but she had also had a number of other things to deal with, obviously.

"Hello." Elsa flared her nostrils as Carmella stepped farther into the office.

"Hey." Carmella clipped the door closed. She hovered far back near the door as though she expected Elsa to demand she leave. "I had a little break between appointments."

Elsa's heart sank. Was Carmella there because of the article? Did she want to rub Elsa's nose in it or, worse, pity her for it? Elsa bit on her lower lip and then said, "What can I do for you, Carmella?" She kept her voice hard-edged.

Carmella slid a strand behind her ear. "Look. I know I'm the last person you want to see right now."

Elsa was immediately struck with her honesty, so much so that she couldn't drum up an immediate response.

"Like everyone else on this stupid rock of an island, I read the article," Carmella admitted.

"Of course, you did." Elsa shrugged flippantly. "You don't read a book for years, but naturally, you read the first bad thing that pops up about my family."

"That's a lie. I read all the time. You don't know anything about me." Carmella's eyebrows lowered dangerously.

Elsa pressed her lips into a thin line. She leaned back in her chair and regarded her younger sister. Yet again, they'd found themselves at war.

"What are you here for, Carmella?"

Carmella rolled her eyes back. "I'm here because — well — because I recognized a few of the names in the article."

Elsa arched an eyebrow and leaned forward against her desk. "What are you talking about?"

"God, you make everything so difficult," Carmella returned.

"Are you going to tell me? Or are you going to yell at me?"

Carmella reached back for the doorknob, and Elsa's heart leaped with fear.

"Hold on. Hold on." Elsa lifted from her chair. "Don't go. Please just tell me."

"I shouldn't have even bothered," Carmella told her.

"I don't even know what you're talking about." Elsa inhaled, then exhaled slowly. "Okay. What names?"

"Some of those men," Carmella said. "The ones pressing charges against Aiden's estate. Your estate, I mean."

"How?"

Carmella pondered for a moment. "We get a lot of women through the Lodge, you know? Some of them stay for many days to pick up the pieces of their lives. Others, they just pass through for massages and mojitos and acupuncture."

"I know our business model, thanks."

Carmella groaned. "You don't have to be sarcastic. I'm just trying to explain."

"Okay. Then explain."

"There are these younger girls that come through. They are addicted to Nancy's massage and my acupuncture. They say they have to do a lot of wining and dining, you know, for their clientele. They said it does horrors to their skin and bodies — which is why they come here. And much like other women who pass through the Lodge, they get pretty chatty."

A fire burned in the back of Elsa's mind.

"Anyway, I have a few of them in tomorrow," Carmella said.

Elsa pressed a hand over her heart. Her eyes connected with Carmella's. "You don't believe Aiden did this, do you?"

Carmella's smile was crooked. It was one of the more beautiful sights Elsa had seen in her life.

"It's not like I was ever close with Aiden," Carmella offered then. "But I always remember this one afternoon. You and Dad and Nancy were on the porch talking and laughing and carrying on like a family should. Mallory and Cole and Alexie were out by the water. And I just felt so lost and between everything else, like I had no place to go. Aiden came up to me and told me this story about when you'd first brought him home with you, and he felt so strange and awkward and out of place. He said that apparently, I had told him a joke, a really awful joke, one that was so awful that he burst into laughter and was finally able to break the ice with Dad and Karen. He said he couldn't believe the nerve of this teenage girl acting so silly. And then he asked me if I was ever silly anymore. I told him I thought maybe I'd lost the capability to be like that. He said that he didn't think that was true— that we can always find a way back to ourselves if we really work for it. Then he walked away."

Carmella furrowed her brow as she spoke. Her eyes filled with tears.

Elsa's own cheeks were damp. She didn't remember the joke Carmella had told as a teenager. She didn't know about this tender moment.

In fact, Aiden had hardly spoken of Carmella at all, as he'd always known she was a sore subject for Elsa.

"I loved him so much, Carmella," Elsa breathed.

Carmella nodded. "I know."

"Why didn't you tell me about this until now?"

Carmella's laugh was terribly sad. "We don't exactly tell each other things, do we?"

Elsa shook her head. She didn't have the strength to speak.

After a long pause, Carmella began again.

"These girls love to brag about these men, their clients. They tell me everything. If I press it, just the tiniest bit, I think I can get them to talk. Maybe they know about Aiden. Maybe they know what's behind all of this."

Elsa swiped at the tears across her cheek. "You would do that?"

Carmella's response was so quiet that Elsa strained to hear her words.

"We're a family, Elsa. In the end, I would do anything for you. I hope you know that."

# Chapter Twenty-One

T he following day, Elsa checked the acupuncture schedule. Sure enough, straight in a line were three women, all of whom had listed themselves as twenty-three years old. Gretchen, Rhea, and Isabella. The two blondes in the bathroom were Gretchen and Rhea — which meant, hopefully, that the red-haired girl was Isabella. Their appointments began at one thirty and stretched until three, with each having a half hour each. Elsa pressed her palms together in prayer. Never in her life had she ever trusted Carmella with anything. Now, she felt as though Carmella held her life in the palm of her hand.

Nancy arrived at her office around one-forty-five. She was a welcomed distraction. She drew her arms over her head and stretched out her spine as she said, "Do you want me to make you a green smoothie? I was thinking about having one for lunch. Janine and I had too much to drink last night, and I have to admit, my body is screaming for nutrients."

Elsa couldn't imagine eating anything; her stomach quaked with nerves.

Nancy dropped her arms to her sides and furrowed her brow. "Has Bruce had any luck with the case?"

Elsa shook her head. "I don't know. I haven't heard from him. I know he's doing the best he can."

"I ran into Susan recently at the store. She spoke about Bruce like he was a genius. 'If anyone could figure this out, it's Bruce,' she said. I hope she's right."

"He's a good man."

"It's incredible that the world can make such excellent men like him and Aiden and Neal and then such horrible men like Janine's father, or these horrible rich sailors."

Elsa wasn't sure what to say. She turned her eyes back toward her hands and willed time to pass. Over the previous year, Nancy had been her backbone; she'd been her everything. Naturally, Nancy could sense the anxiety within her.

"You'll tell me if you need something. Won't you?" Nancy finally asked.

Elsa lifted her eyes. "Of course."

"That's a lie if I've ever heard one," Nancy told her.

Elsa grimaced. "You know I'll be fine."

Behind Nancy, Mallory called out to say that Nancy's two fifteen had already arrived and could be taken earlier if she had the time. Nancy nodded again to Elsa and said, "Please, remember I'm here for you. We have to be there for each other. There's no other way."

"I remember. Thank you, Nancy." After another pause, Elsa added, "I love you."

"I love you, too, Sugar."

Elsa felt completely stricken after Nancy's departure. She wandered back and forth in her office, both dreading and aching for the moment that Carmella would arrive. She half imagined Carmella bursting in, laughing outrageously, and saying, "It's true what they said! Aiden really did do it! He's a damn thief! He's been evil all this time, and you didn't know it! You're such an idiot!"

*But no. That was crazy, wasn't it?*

All she had were her memories; how awful to feel them slipping into darkness.

At three ten, there was a knock on the door. Elsa lurched for the handle and yanked it open to find Carmella before her. Her eyes glittered strangely. Elsa beckoned for her to enter as though they were in the midst of a covert operation. She felt like they were spies.

With the door closed, Carmella and Elsa stood looking at one another. The silence was deafening. Elsa still struggled to read Carmella's expression. Slowly, a smile trickled across her lips.

"Well? What happened?" Elsa finally demanded.

Carmella lifted her phone from her pocket. She placed it flat on her palm.

Elsa raised an eyebrow.

"I recorded it," Carmella said simply.

Elsa's eyes nearly bugged from her skull. "No. That's totally illegal. It's —"

"Not as illegal as what they were doing, Elsa." Carmella's face grew hard. "Listen. Okay? Just listen."

Carmella dotted a finger on the PLAY button. In a moment, the red-haired girl's voice sprung up through the speakers.

At first, there was the necessary introduction. Carmella's voice began with, "And we've done all this before, so you know what to expect. The first little prick and then —"

"Yeah, yeah." The red-haired girl, Isabella, sounded flippant. "No worries at all. Just take me back to that beautiful, relaxing space, Carmella! You're a goddess!"

Slowly, their conversation trickled into other things. As

Carmella stuck Isabella with needles, her speech became softer, more nuanced, more reflective.

"It's been such a strange summer," Isabella breathed. "Like, just a little over a year ago, I was still living in that tiny room in Queens. I mean, can you imagine me now, in Queens?"

The recording of Carmella admitted that she couldn't.

"I was miserable. But this older woman I met at the little cafe I worked at told me about this app that paired you up with rich men. I swear I got so lucky too because I spoke with some girls who said they met several men who were unkind or unwilling to extend the relationship further or were only in it for the goods, you know."

The recording of Carmella said this was all fascinating, that she wanted to know more. "Things are so different than they were back when I was younger. Maybe I would have done something similar," she said.

Elsa blinked up at the current version of Carmella. "Would you have really done that?"

Carmella shook her head. "No way. I just wanted Isabella to feel like she could open up to me more."

The recording continued.

"Me and Carlson just have this really deep connection. Have you ever had that with someone?"

Carmella's recorded voice admitted that she'd had very few connections in her life.

This, in turn, made Elsa's heart ache for her sister.

"That's too bad," Isabella said. "I mean, everyone thinks the age difference is weird, and of course, there's the fact that he pays me. But after a while, it wasn't about the money. Not for either of us. And I've helped him so much with his business. I mean, in a way, it's like we're partners in crime."

Carmella said that sounded beautiful. She didn't press for more details. Instead, she artfully created an ecosystem in which Isabella wanted to tell more. People loved to talk about themselves. She was on a roll.

"I mean, you should really see the way we work together. It's like magic. He's made his money through a lot of different means, but he's never had me. He calls me his secret weapon. We've traveled from island to island together doing this. We hang out at various local bars with all these sailors. He's known how to sail since he was a kid, so he's a part of this world too, but he's also an outsider.

"Over the years, he's worked with a number of stockbrokers and various businessmen— countless, really. He showed me the paperwork, and it turns out, a few of these men he's worked with have actually passed away."

Suddenly, Elsa's brain turned to fire. Her eyes jumped to Carmella's. Carmella nodded firmly. This was real.

"Anyway, and oh my God, I can't believe I'm telling you this —"

"Who am I going to tell?" the recorded voice of Carmella asked.

"Totally. I mean, you know that a girl has to make money where she can," Isabella said.

"That's right," the recording of Carmella said.

"Anyway, we track down these widows and make up these stories about their husbands, that they swindled Carlson. That they set up bad investments for Carlson. Carlson is the legal and business mastermind behind all of it, but I help track them down. It's so much fun. I always say he's like James Bond, and I'm — well — you know, one of those hot James Bond girls. Like, um, Halle Berry was one, wasn't she? Anyway, it's been so fun. We're in the middle of a few projects right now. Carlson can't get enough. He's so high off the power."

Carmella stopped the recording.

There, Elsa and Carmella stood, gaping at one another. Elsa literally couldn't speak. Her mind was racing with the information she just listened to and her heart hammered in her chest. She looked at Carmela feeling the tears that threatened to roll down her cheeks, and she swallowed the lump in her throat before finally asking, "Is this real?"

Carmella nodded. "It sure is."

"She just spilled the beans— all of it like she didn't have a care in the world or half a brain for that matter."

Carmella shrugged. "People say almost anything when they have needles in them. It's weird."

Suddenly, Elsa flung herself forward and wrapped her arms around her younger sister. A sob rushed from her throat, and tears rolled down her cheeks. Slowly, Carmella drew her own arms around Elsa and held on to her tightly. There they stood, two sisters who had spent most of their lives as far apart as they could. Elsa leaned heavily upon her, so much so that Carmella nearly lost her balance and teetered. This made both of them laugh despite their tears.

When Elsa stepped back, she reeled with shock. "I can't believe that you got her to confess all of this. You did it, Carmella. You cleared Aiden's name, our name."

Carmella's smile was electric. It was proof beyond anything that all she had wanted to do was show her love for her sister. She wanted to fight for her family.

"Come with me. We have to show this to Bruce," Elsa said.

Carmella nodded. "I'll drive."

# Chapter Twenty-Two

Bruce's face was stoic. He clasped his hands beneath his chin and listened once, then again, as Isabella explained what she and Carlson Montague had been up to. He then turned his eyes toward Carmella and Elsa — a pair of sisters he had assuredly never seen together and said, point-blank, "You know this is illegal, right?"

Carmella's shrug was flippant. "You think I care? They were dragging my brother-in-law's name through the mud. I would have done anything."

Elsa's smile was electric after that. Bruce matched hers. Elsa had the funniest feeling that, if she was happy, Bruce reflected that. He lifted a pen and began to scribble notes to himself on a yellow notepad. Throughout, Carmella reached over and squeezed Elsa's hand. It was as though the two of them had been to war together; they had stories reaching as far back as forty years before. Now, they had put aside their differences for this common goal. And dammit, maybe they had succeeded. Time would tell the tale.

"I obviously can't use this recording as evidence," Bruce

finally said as he lifted his chin. "But it does give me a direction. I'm going to look into other lawsuits this Carlson guy is putting out there. Build a case around that. And of course, I'll know what kind of questions to ask Isabella. It seems like she's cracked around the edges. It'll be even worse if this Carlson guy ever dumps her. I'm sure she'll be like a faucet."

Elsa squeezed her eyes shut. Suddenly, there was light at the end of this horrifically dark tunnel; suddenly, she felt there was hope.

"Thank you, Bruce," Elsa said. "I can't even tell you how much your work on this has meant to me."

The word "work" seemed silly; it seemed to only encapsulate about ten percent of their time together. In truth, he had been much more like a friend, even as the world had spun off its axis even further.

Bruce walked them out to the foyer. He shook their hands and said he was "on it" and that he would send word as soon as he knew more. Elsa and Carmella walked into the shimmering light of the late July afternoon. It was the final day of the month, and in mere days, the Katama Lodge would hold a celebration for the success of its first few weeks since re-opening. Elsa felt light as a feather. Her legs sprung beneath her as she walked. She was in such high spirits that she could have floated home.

"Why don't we get a glass of wine?" Elsa suddenly suggested. She couldn't remember the last time she had ever purposely tried to spend time with her sister, one-on-one.

Carmella didn't miss a beat. "Let's try that new winery near the Hesson House that's located along the water."

"Perfect."

* * *

Carmella drove them toward the Hesson House, Olivia Hesson's newly-opened boutique hotel. It had already been written up with rave reviews in several magazines, including *The New Yorker* and *The Atlantic*, with a full-page spread interview with Olivia, who had recounted beautiful stories with her great-aunt, who had left her the hotel after she'd passed.

The little winery was located about five hundred feet from the hotel and it burst out from the tree line and dipped across the beautiful sands. Carmella and Elsa walked slowly toward the furthest table from the inside; they didn't have to discuss it — they just wanted to be as near to the waves as they could.

Elsa hadn't been on a "first date" with someone since she'd met Aiden a million years before. Somehow, though, her stomach jumped and shivered in a way that reminded her of first-date jitters. Funny, since she sat at a table now with her actual blood-related sister.

"What kind of wine should we get? It's on me," Elsa said.

They opted for a bottle of rose from Provence. When the server left, Elsa realized that she had absolutely no idea what to say to this beautiful woman. She folded and unfolded her hands on her lap. Again, she thought of their mother, Tina, and how Carmella was startlingly exactly like her during her last years.

"Thank you again for everything. I don't know how we would have gotten all that information without you."

Carmella nodded. She seemed at a loss for words, too. They'd had such a rush of emotion, of glory and now, they were again left with the strange, amorphous relationship between them. The server arrived shortly with their glasses of wine, and Elsa lifted hers to clink with Carmella's.

"I guess this cheers is to justice."

"To justice," Carmella echoed. "They better not mess with the Remington girls again."

"No. They better not." Elsa sipped her wine and then turned her eyes toward the water. In the distance, a bird landed on the glow of the somber sea just as another wave rushed toward it. It fluttered away quickly in the nick of time.

"Why did you decide to help me, Carmella?" Elsa's question was a surprise even to herself.

Carmella dropped her eyes toward her wine. She then sipped it — perhaps more than she meant to, then slid her hand over her lips. After a long pause, she said, "I've never seen anyone look as miserable as you have the last year. That is, anyone besides myself when I look in the mirror every morning. But I'm used to looking like that. I'm not used to my older, beautiful, confident sister looking like that and it killed me."

Elsa, who'd never imagined her sister had even regarded her with any emotion like that at all, was taken aback.

Her voice cracked with her response.

"I should have done something about us all these years, Carmella. I hate that I let things go on for so long like they have."

Again, Carmella couldn't meet Elsa's eye. She sipped her wine again. A few tables away, a young man babbled through what sounded like a first date. He literally couldn't stop bragging about himself. Maybe, if Elsa had been at the wine bar with an actual friend rather than her sister, she might have joked about him. But here, her tongue felt so flat.

"I just feel like Karen did way more damage than either of us realized," Elsa continued.

At this, Carmella's eyes snapped up to Elsa's. Resentment fell over her face.

"I mean, come on, Carmella. Don't you remember all the stuff she used to say to you about me? Not all of it was true."

Still, Carmella didn't speak. Elsa felt anxious and she scrambled to say the right thing.

"I mean, I know you like, loved her, or whatever, but listen, she tore our family apart," she continued.

Dark shadows formed beneath Carmella's eyes.

"And, did you ever even hear from her again after she left?" Elsa demanded. "I mean, she always said you two were best friends, but where was she when Dad kicked her out? Where was she when Dad's money was no longer at play? Huh?"

Carmella snapped her hand across the table so hard that the wine shook back and forth in their glasses. Her eyes were ominous.

"Why the hell do you have to bring this up, huh? You really know how to kill the mood."

Elsa's lips formed a thin line, and her eyes grew large with shock.

"I mean, why do you want to beat an old horse? Over and over again? Isn't it enough that you and Nancy have your little club together? Now, I guess you have Janine, too. A new sister, one with no relation to Karen or to Colton or to Mom or to anything that hurts you from the past."

"Nobody said anything about Mom or Colton," Elsa returned.

"Yeah? Well. Here, I'm bringing them out for you. All our ghosts, Elsa. And in all of it, you never wanted me to be happy. You and Dad and Mom were always content for me to just live in the guilt of what I'd done. Now, I do one nice thing for you, and you want to dance all over the Karen issue again. Whatever, you know? I don't want to deal with it. I'm glad your precious family name is probably saved. But it's clear to me, more than ever, that I was happy with the way things were between us."

Carmella leaped from her chair and stormed off across the beach. She disappeared between the shadows of the trees, enraged. Elsa rushed after her, but Carmella's long legs had already snaked her all the way back to her car. In a flash, she was gone. Elsa remained in the darkness of the forest as the rush of the wind and the sound of the waves fell over her. Yet again, she staggered through another problem with her sister.

It seemed increasingly clear that they would never be able to fix the trauma between them.

They would never find common ground.

Elsa returned to the table and watched the waves mold over the sand, shifting it, molding it in ways that would alter a million times over in the course of a month. She lifted her phone exactly once in an attempt to write something meaningful to Carmella.

But there was nothing to say. She couldn't change the past. It felt impossible.

# Chapter Twenty-Three

T he Katama Lodge and Wellness Spa celebration was held on the first Saturday in August. The air simmered with excitement as the white tent ballooned up toward the glowing blue sky in preparation; the kitchen sizzled with new recipes, as the chef hustled to keep up with everything and ordered the various new hires to "fry this" or "bake that." The women who'd chosen to stay at the Lodge these days came out of their suites and cabins in a haze. After all, they'd spent their time meditating, getting massages, speaking to therapists, and getting acupuncture — their minds were in the midst of reformation. They were like caterpillars in their cocoons, preparing to become butterflies.

Elsa hustled about the grounds, grateful to have something to do with her hands. She had a great deal to think about, and any time she spent at her desk meant rolling thoughts of panic and fear. Bruce was still in the midst of his investigation; the island still gossiped about Aiden and spread misinformation about his good name, and Carmella still wouldn't look her in the eye after their fight at the winery. It was as though everything had the possibility to be great, but Elsa just wasn't sure how to make the greatness flourish.

The party began at eight. Everyone on Martha's Vineyard knew that Katama Lodge knew how to throw parties, and soon there was an influx of some of the greatest islanders — Jennifer Conrad, Olivia Hesson, Camilla Jenkins, Lola, Christine, and Susan Sheridan, and a number of other beautiful and prominent men and women who made the community such a marvelous one.

Elsa snaked through the crowd and spotted Mallory off toward the trees, which lined the grounds. Mallory had decided on a light pink dress with a tender line of beautiful buttons that trailed from the neck toward her knees. Her hair shined beneath the sun, but her face lent a far different expression of anger and sorrow.

Elsa followed her daughter's line of sight to find none other than Lucas. He stood in a pair of slacks and a button-down shirt with a bouquet outstretched in his arms. Mallory crossed her arms over her chest as Lucas spoke. Elsa burned with a desire to go over there and save her daughter from more heartache.

But her daughter was twenty-four years old. She was a mother, and she had to fight her own battles. She had to make her own decisions, just as Elsa always had before her.

Just then, there was a soft tap on Elsa's shoulder. She stepped over and twisted her head, falling from her reverie.

There, far above her, was a pair of soft green eyes.

"Bruce." She couldn't help it as a smile stretched from ear to ear. "I had no idea you were coming tonight."

Bruce was dressed wonderfully. He wore a pair of dark jeans and a polo shirt, which highlighted his muscles wonderfully. He had a beer in hand, and that same cologne came off him in a soft wave.

Beyond anything, the look in his eyes made her feel something. Wanted, maybe. Adored.

Not that either of them would ever do anything about it. They were both grieving.

And in that way, both understood the other much more than ever needed to be said, maybe.

"I couldn't miss it," Bruce said finally. "And my brother and sister told me you guys always have the best parties. I have to admit that this is one of the better views of the Bay. And the grounds are just gorgeous."

Elsa's heart swelled with pride. "Not everyone is lucky enough to have a family business like this. I definitely count my blessings every day."

Bruce nodded and held her gaze. "Can I grab you a beer or something?" he finally asked.

"Oh! Um, wine, please." Elsa turned her eyes back toward Mallory, where she caught the first sign of an actual smile on her daughter's face.

Was it possible that Lucas would win her back?

Even after everything that had happened?

Oh, but wasn't that a good thing? Shouldn't Elsa want Zachery's father in his life?

"That's my daughter," Elsa said suddenly, just before Bruce headed off to grab her wine. "And her ex-fiancé."

Bruce groaned. "Ex? That sounds like a mess."

"Yep. Sure is. Although... I don't know. They seem happy? Dare I say it?"

Bruce laughed good-naturedly. "They're young. They're good at making messes."

"I was so stable back then. I was twenty-four years old, with three babies, a husband, and a career."

"I don't think it's healthy to compare," Bruce said tentatively. "Everyone is on their own journey, and your daughter will find her way."

Elsa chuckled. "I don't mean to say that she's late to her

journey or lagging. I'm just saying that I feel just about as lost as Mallory does now. No journey is linear."

"No journey is linear. Wiser words have never been spoken."

Elsa turned her eyes back toward his. They held one another's gaze for a long, beautiful moment.

"I want to go over there and tell him he's not good enough for my daughter."

Bruce's crooked smile was endearing. "But you won't?"

Elsa shook her head. She then swallowed the lump in her throat and continued. "When I was younger, I tried as hard as I could to meddle in my little sister's business. She resented me for it. There are, of course, so many other factors at play—decades and decades of hardships. But I'm not sure she'll ever forgive me, and that tears me up. I would hate for Mallory to feel that I had somehow messed up a good thing. All I can do is offer love and support. Especially now."

Bruce furrowed his brow. "When you and your sister were in my office, I couldn't help but notice —"

Elsa arched an eyebrow as silence filled the space after his words. "Notice what?"

"Just how similar you two are. All your mannerisms and the way your eyebrows jump up when you find something funny. Even the way you laugh. It's uncanny. I suppose it must have been the way your mother was. I hope it's not too much for me to say that."

Tears sprung to Elsa's eyes. All this time, she had regarded Carmella as the living portrait of their mother, Tina. She had never imagined that Tina lived on in her, too.

"Anyway, I'll grab you that wine," Bruce said delicately as he spread his palm across the back of his neck.

"Bruce." Elsa drew her own hand over his wrist. It was such a tender motion, one that surprised even Elsa herself. "Thank you for saying that. And for helping us as much as you have. I don't even have the right words to say. So thank you."

When Bruce returned with her glass of wine, Elsa was in a bubbling conversation with Jennifer Conrad and her handsome developer boyfriend, Derek. Bruce and Derek struck up a lovely friendship, the kind that focused on fishing and sailing outings and how good they were at golf. Jennifer and Elsa rolled their eyes and shared playful smiles.

Bruce and Elsa lost one another later on. Elsa tended to a few small disasters in the kitchen, chatted with Nancy for a while about the success of the party, and even danced on the dance floor with Janine and her friend, Henry, who seemed overly willing to place his hand on the small of her back and draw her close. Janine's eyes were electric with the joy of it all. She looked like a giddy teenager.

Mallory met her on the dance floor during a softer number. A local guitarist sat center stage with his acoustic across his lap and strummed beautifully with long fingers.

"I saw Lucas," Elsa finally said.

Mallory nodded as she leaned against the wall. "He wants to spend a bit of time as a family. Just the three of us. He said that he's started going to therapy to address some of his problems."

"Wow." Elsa certainly hadn't expected Lucas to actually step up and handle his demons head-on.

"I told him we have a really hard road ahead of us and that we have to have open and honest communication. That we need to do everything we can for Zachery even if that means separating for good."

"You sound wise beyond your years, honey. I'm really proud of you."

"I guess you have to be when you have a kid. But I guess you already know that."

"Wiser and much younger. Maybe you never feel the exact

age you are," Elsa said. "Just promise me, you'll put yourself first before everything. You're doing pretty darn okay without Lucas around."

"It's remarkable to know that I can live without him. I think I was so eager, you know, to have babies and get married. I never fully considered what it might mean to be alone or that it would happen."

Elsa, who had spent the first year of her life alone the previous year, nodded knowingly. It was incredible in a sense, realizing that you could be alone. It wasn't discussed; it had never been a part of many women's narratives.

As twilight flung flickering stars across the sky, Elsa ambled toward the edge of the party, where Bruce towered over many with one hand in his pocket and the other gripping a beer. He looked contemplative yet content. She was drawn to him like a moth to a flame.

"Having fun?" she asked him.

He jumped slightly at the sight of her. Elsa wondered if he'd been thinking about her. Was that too presumptuous?

"It's a great party," he complimented. "I have to admit. I haven't let myself let loose in a while."

"I get that. It's difficult for me, too."

"We should try to push ourselves to be more open to that stuff," Bruce said. "Make sure we're still having fun despite everything else."

Elsa nodded. Again, a lump formed in her throat.

"By the way, I wanted to tell you. I've been in conversation with a journalist in New York," Bruce continued. His eyes shifted out toward the water. "What Carlson Montague has been doing is a huge scandal. And it seems like a huge article might be coming out that will crack this thing wide open and clear Aiden's name."

"Bruce..." Elsa was overcome with emotion. She batted her eyes quickly, trying to keep her tears at bay. This was certainly not the time or place. "Bruce, that means the world to me."

Bruce nodded. He then turned his eyes toward the ground as he said, "Knowing you, the past few weeks have been remarkable. I feel awake in ways I never thought I would."

"I feel that, too."

"Then you probably also feel the other stuff," Bruce said softly.

"That it's too soon?"

"Yes," Bruce said.

Elsa nodded. Sorrow swirled with joy and crafted a tornado in her gut. How horrendously difficult all of life was! There was never a moment of rest.

Bruce's eyes twinkled as he added, "But that doesn't mean I want to stop seeing you. Even after the case is closed."

"Me neither." The thought of not seeing Bruce any longer actually filled her with dread. She suddenly felt like a temperamental teenager. She slid a strand of hair behind her ear and imagined them kissing right then beneath the budding moonlight. "I really mean that," she said, as though those words added anything at all.

Bruce bid her good night after that. Elsa watched as his shadow flickered out along the line of trees until his form disappeared into the amorphous darkness. When she closed her eyes, however, her mind turned back to Aiden and her consciousness spoke to him. *"If you can hear me, if you can see me, know that I still love you with everything I am. But I'm still on this earth, and I still have time to live. Maybe I'll find a way to do that."*

# Chapter Twenty-Four

The party guests departed just after midnight. Elsa's throat grew hoarse as she called out to so many, "Thank you for coming! The Lodge wouldn't be the same without you." As she stood with her hand raised mid-wave, an arm stretched over her shoulder and held her close. Nancy's perfume and the slightest hint of wine-laced breath fell over her. Elsa turned her face to dot her nose against her stepmother's.

"What a party, huh?" Nancy said. Her words were passionate and meant as a compliment. She then kissed her stepdaughter on the cheek and said, "I think it's time for the four of us Lodge girls to have a little meeting."

Elsa arched an eyebrow. "We have a meeting next week. Tuesday afternoon, right?"

"Not that kind of meeting," Nancy corrected. "This is the kind of meeting that demands moonlight."

Nancy led Elsa out toward the dock, which stretched out on the southernmost side of the Katama Lodge's beach area, nearest to one of their larger rented cabins. There, already awaiting them, stood Janine and Carmella. Elsa had kept her distance from Carmella throughout the party; in fact, she had thought her sister had left hours before because she hadn't spotted her. Now, she stood with her arms crossed too tightly over her chest as her skirt whipped around her. The sea breeze made her look entirely whimsical — like a beautiful prom queen. Elsa longed to tell her that. She longed to tell her so many things.

She was really sorry for all of it.

"Girls! Let's gather on the edge of the dock," Nancy instructed. She stepped out on the creaking boards as the waves stirred beneath them.

The water was impenetrable, so dark that it filled Elsa's stomach with fear. She followed Nancy out to the edge and listened as Janine and Carmella came close behind. Out there, they stood in a single line with their noses pointed toward the water. The moon cast a ghoulish light over them. For a moment, Elsa had the funniest idea that they would all join hands and leap into the abyss and swim out into the night — maybe become mermaids and never return to their chaotic lives.

"I wanted to gather you girls out here tonight for a sort of ceremony," Nancy said softly. "We've worked alongside one another for the previous few weeks, and we've had ups and downs and trials along the way. Still, I feel it in my bones. We will be doing this together for a long time. We will be assisting so, so many women through trauma and pain and hardship. It is what we were put on this earth to do.

"But in order to do that, I feel that we all must work harder on ourselves. We must focus on our own hardship and pain and work, day after day, to alleviate our own darkness. I can feel them in all of us. And here, beneath the moon, I want us all to express them. I want us to state our deepest, darkest fears. If we cast them out over the water, they can't hurt us any longer. We'll have total power over them.

"Anyway. I'll go first," Nancy breathed. She then reached through the space between herself and Elsa and clutched her hand. Elsa followed suit and found her own hand latched with Carmella's.

She couldn't remember the last time they'd held hands, maybe when they'd been very small.

Carmella then took Janine's hand on the other side. Together, they formed a powerful link.

"So many years ago, I was a black hole of a person," Nancy began. "I used people for my own advantage. I lost money, time, ego, and health. I gave so much of myself to things that didn't matter at all, and that resulted in losing my beautiful daughter. Then I lost a number of careers, places to live, and my friends. By the time I met Neal, I had mastered the art of losing.

"But Neal taught me so much about the world, about acceptance, about life and love. When he brought me to the island, I thought — *I don't deserve this chance.* It wasn't even a second chance. It was more like my twelfth or thirteenth chance. I told him that, too. And he told me, Nancy, let me love you. Let Elsa love you. Let Carmella love you."

Beside Elsa, Carmella made the smallest of noises in her throat. Elsa wondered what it meant. Was it a protest to Nancy's proclamation that Carmella loved her at all?

"I lost that man last year, but I've gained so much along the way. I am forever grateful for him, and my only fear is that I won't be strong enough to live in the things he taught me forever. But I suppose that's why my daughter is here. That's why my stepdaughters, his daughters, are here. They are my guiding lights in the darkness, and I love you all so dearly."

Nancy then squeezed Elsa's hand. It was her turn to speak.

Elsa heaved a sigh.

"I've lost so much over the past year," she whispered. "And like Nancy, I wonder how I can maintain all that love enough to give it to the people we meet along the way. I'm terrified that I won't be enough for my daughters or my son. Or our clients. Or my stepmother. Or my new stepsister. Or... my sister, who I love so much."

Carmella squeezed Elsa's hand hard. A jolt of electricity seemed to pass between them.

"I want to be enough all the time. But I know I've made and will continue to make every mistake in the book. But all I need to do is keep trying, and I pledge that I will forever."

It was Carmella's turn. But she shook her head strangely as she closed her eyes tight. Maybe it was too much for her. Maybe she just didn't have anything to say.

Janine went next. She spoke of everything she had lost in Manhattan and how that loss had filled her with a sense of dread that perhaps she wasn't good enough to hold on to happiness. "I want to fight every day to be the kind of woman our clients and you three, along with my daughters, can rely on."

After a pause, Nancy cleared her throat and lifted her chin still more toward the moon. "We project our anxieties and fears out across the waters, and we receive goodwill from the universe. United we stand, stronger than ever in light and in love."

Nancy dropped Elsa's hand. She then turned back and walked somberly down the dock. Janine followed after her, which left only the two Remington girls at the very edge of the creaking dock. Their hands remained latched together. Elsa didn't dare let Carmella go.

"I just couldn't speak in front of the other two," Carmella suddenly said. "Maybe that means I'm the most afraid of all of us. I can't even speak my fears out loud to the universe because then I'll have to face them head-on."

"Fears are fears no matter how loud you shout them," Elsa murmured. "And you know, you can tell me if you want to.

Whatever you need. Or we can just stand here. I don't really mind."

Carmella cleared her throat. After a long moment, she whispered, "I'm afraid I'll never be able to find a way back to you."

Elsa sniffed. "Me too."

"There's just so much pain between us. I know you're right about so much of the Karen stuff. It's just been so ingrained in my story for so dang long. I find it difficult to see beyond it."

"Of course. It only makes sense."

"And all the other stuff with Colton and Mom and Dad. I mean. Gosh, Elsa. What kind of deal did I make with the universe? Why has it been so bad for so long?"

"I wish there was an answer."

Carmella squeezed Elsa's hand still harder. "Can you be patient with me, Elsa? While I work through all of this? While I find a way back to you?"

"Only if you'll be patient with me."

"Because we're bound to fight. We always fight."

"We really do."

"It's one of the only things I'm really good at — fighting with you," Carmella said.

Elsa chuckled. "I think you have an infinite number of talents. The fighting with me thing is just one of them."

They held the silence again. Elsa felt the enormity of their love for one another. It swelled out from them and created a kind of orb of protection around them.

"Do you remember that night we went swimming with Colton?" Carmella asked. "I guess he was nine or something. And we rushed off this very dock and into the dark water. Mom nearly had a heart attack."

Elsa laughed. "I couldn't understand why she didn't trust me to take care of you guys. I kept telling her, 'I was there, Mom! Everything was fine!' But I was just a kid, too."

Suddenly, Carmella yanked her skirt down to her ankles and removed her tank top. She stood in only her bra and underwear and wagged her eyebrows. "Are you up for this, Elsa Remington Steel?"

Elsa's laughter twinkled out across the bay. She followed suit and soon stood in her bra and panties.

"On the count of three, we jump in. Hand in hand," Carmella said.

"Okay."

"One," Carmella began.

"Two," said Elsa.

And then, they both cried out, "THREE," as they leaped into the dark abyss beyond the dock. Their fingers lost grip on one another the moment they shot through the warm Bay waters. And when they rushed back to the air above, their laughter was youthful, jovial, and every bit as light as it had been so many years before when Colton had been with them.

# Chapter Twenty-Five

**M**allory and Elsa were next in line at the Frosted Delights bakery. It had been two days since the party at Katama Lodge, and still, the island seemed abuzz with excitement and stories about the event. Even now at the bakery, Elsa heard several mentions of the décor, the food, the music, and the bits of drama that had, of course, flourished at the party. The island profited off its gossip; it needed to create enough of it to get through the chilly winter months. It was the only way they all survived on that rock in the middle of the sea.

"I hope Lucas is okay," Mallory breathed as she glanced out the window. Anxiety permeated her face.

"I'm sure he is," Elsa returned, having decided that positivity was the only way forward when it came to her ex-future-son-in-law. "He's great with the baby when he wants to be. And right now, he really wants to be."

Mallory beamed; her eyes echoed her gratefulness. "He's a good dad. And he could be a good partner. I told him we have all the time in the world to figure ourselves out. We just have to give Zachery a beautiful day, every day. And if he wants to be a part of that, he can be. I won't stand in his way."

In the meantime, however, Mallory had decided to stay at Nancy's place. There was more than enough space, and the warmth of their ever-growing family flowed from room to room. It was addicting. Elsa felt this way, too. Still, a small voice in the back of her mind had begun to question what she might do with her and Aiden's house. It just sat there, a big shell of a place, an empty vessel of memories. Perhaps one day, she would sell it. Perhaps she would find the strength to rent it out. Who knew?

Of course, there was the issue of potential new lives — with Bruce Holland or otherwise. Perhaps she would want the space for a fresh start. She wasn't sure yet. And there was beauty in the uncertainty. She had to see that, too.

"What can I get you, girls?" Jennifer Conrad beamed at them over the counter as the two selected a number of donuts to bring back to the Katama Lodge for Nancy, Janine, and Carmella. Elsa pointed at a number of delectable options — chocolate-glazed and maple-icing and cream-stuffed. Jennifer loaded up a box, and Mallory took it in hand and thanked her.

"Really great party the other night," Jennifer added as Elsa leafed through her purse for a ten-dollar bill. "I could hang out on the Katama Lodge grounds all day. It's just so beautiful!"

Elsa and Mallory turned back toward the door. In the rush of it, Elsa's eyes landed on a newspaper held upright by a man who sipped black coffee and nibbled on a donut.

The headline read: **MILLIONAIRE SAILOR CONNED WIDOWS FOR HUNDREDS OF THOU-SANDS OF DOLLARS**

Elsa all but leaped over to the man. He shifted the paper away from himself and furrowed his brow.

"Can I borrow that newspaper?" she asked hurriedly. She felt like a little kid.

"Um... Sure?" He passed it to her, and she flashed back to the front page.

"Carlson Montague seems to be your traditional million-aire: property across the world, twentysomething women hanging off his every word (and his pocketbook), money to burn, and relationships to mishandle. He leaps aboard his yacht every summer and travels from island to island, making a mockery of poor folks who scrape together enough funds for rent every month.

"But there's something incredibly amiss about Carlson Montague, something that only comes after a bit of necessary digging. You see, Carlson Montague might have made his first million honestly — or at least semi-honestly. But since then, he's pushed his luck, operating in illegal dealings and offshore accounts, and even pressing widows of various stockbrokers and businessmen, stating that their husbands mishandled his funds and demanding a huge amount of funds. Take Aiden Steel of Martha's Vineyard, for example..."

Elsa's hands shook so hard that the paper shivered and rustled against itself.

"Mom?" Mallory popped up beside her and glanced at the paper. "Oh my God. Is this...?"

"I didn't expect that it would happen so soon." Elsa's throat tightened. "This is incredible. This—"

"Just take it," the man with the newspaper said. "I can pick up a new one." He returned his attention to his donut as though he'd already forgotten about her. Elsa wanted to laugh aloud.

Outside, Elsa placed the paper on top of her car and continued to read in the early August sunlight. When she'd reread it again, she lifted her phone and dialed Bruce's number. Mallory sipped her coffee and looked at her mother with a mix of worry and happiness.

"Hey, there. I wondered when I'd hear from you," Bruce said.

Elsa's laughter rang out. "I can't believe it. I just keep reading it."

"The journalist discovered some pretty damning facts about our man Carlson, along with a number of his associates. I've already received word that Carlson is dropping the lawsuit against you. I imagine he will be taken to court by the women he's wronged already."

"That's just incredible. I really can't believe this. Bruce, thank you. From the bottom of my heart. Thank you."

"You know, I would have done it for any of my clients. But I'm glad I could do it for you. Really glad."

They held the silence for a moment. Elsa's heart swelled.

"I think we should celebrate," Elsa said suddenly. "Why don't you come to the house tonight? We'll have a barbecue, and you can hang with my family. I know Aiden would have wanted that. Please."

It didn't take long for Bruce to agree. It was decided he would arrive at seven. Elsa dropped her phone back in her purse and leaped up and down like a teenage girl. "He's innocent. We're out of this stupid mess! Nobody will try to take advantage of this family ever again. Not as long as Bruce Holland has anything to say about it," she cried.

\* \* \*

Cole arrived at Nancy's house with a massive stack of newspapers. "I couldn't buy enough of them," he explained with a huge grin. He smacked the stack on the back porch table and then wrapped his thick, muscular arms around his mother. "I'm just so glad it's over. I heard so many people talking about it today. At the grocery store. At the docks. Nobody can believe that someone tried to drag Dad's name through the mud. And suddenly, everyone has a great story about him to tell. Suddenly, he's the greatest person who ever lived, all over again."

"He always was, to begin with. People are just difficult. They believe what they want to believe," Elsa said with a sad shrug.

The doorbell rang just then, and Elsa's heart leaped into her throat. But after a moment, Lucas appeared from the shadows of the interior of the house, carrying baby Zachery. Mallory leaped up and greeted them warmly. She took the baby in her arms and lifted her beautiful eyes to the man she still loved. "How was it?"

"It was great," Lucas replied. "My mom freaked out, having him around. She just dotes on him." As he entered the porch, he waved a hand toward everyone, including Elsa. He looked sheepish; he knew he'd messed up.

Still, Elsa told her heart to find a way to forgive him.

Just then, another figure appeared behind Lucas. Carmella rushed out through the screen door with a wine bottle raised. She beamed at Elsa. "I can't stop reading that crazy article! I can't believe it. And do you think that 'secret source' he talks about is Isabella?"

"It has to be," Elsa affirmed as she jumped up to hug her. "And sis, we couldn't have done any of this without you. You were the secret ingredient."

Nancy rushed out from the kitchen carrying a large bowl of guacamole and a bag of chips, which she placed at the center of the table. She clasped her hands as she said, "I have the barbecue all heated up and the guac's made. I think it's time for margaritas? Cole, I'm going to need you to start on the burgers here soon because I'm famished."

"Aye aye, captain," Cole said brightly.

"All this sailor talk has me hungry, too," Carmella said as she slid into the chair across from Elsa. "Where's Janine, anyway?"

Suddenly, Elsa spotted Janine on the far end of the beach. She walked hand in hand with none other than Henry. As they walked along, Janine dropped her head back, erupting with laughter. Elsa's heart surged with happiness for them. It was a budding friendship, a tender romance. And maybe it would even last.

But Janine deserved every happiness in the world.

Nancy delivered them scrumptious margaritas. Elsa dipped a chip into the top of the guacamole and nibbled slowly. All the while, she kept focusing on the shadows inside the house. Bruce had said he would arrive at seven, and it was now five minutes past.

Had he decided whatever brewed between them was too much too soon for him?

Had he decided to take a massive step back?

It would be understandable if he didn't want to be friends. Elsa could handle it. She had enough love in her life, and she knew that everyone, from Nancy to Janine, to Carmella, to Bruce — needed to handle their trauma and pain in his or her own way. Still, she would have loved to lend strength to his heart. She would have loved to be a listening ear, a soft touch.

She would have loved to try to love again— eventually.

Cole smacked the pink burger patties onto the grill. They sizzled brightly as Cole said, "I just love that smell!" He then turned mischievously toward Mallory as he said, "Are you still a veg-head, Mal? I always forget where you're at with that."

"She hasn't been vegetarian for years," Lucas said with a laugh. "Ever since we went to the diner, and you said you would lose your mind if you didn't eat a Reuben sandwich. Remember?"

Mallory blushed. "I loved being a vegetarian, but I just couldn't hack it for long. Not like you, Aunt Carmella."

"I only do a few vegetarian days a week these days," Carmella confessed. "And I don't think I'll be able to resist that burger. Especially with the goat cheese I brought from the dairy farm." She drew out the package from her purse and beamed.

"You're evil, Carm," Elsa said with a laugh. "I would eat my weight in that if you'd let me."

Suddenly, the front doorbell buzzed. Elsa knew beyond anything that this was Bruce — her knight in shining armor. She rushed from her chair and bounded into the house. She was reminded of long ago when Aiden had first come to this very house to pick her up for their first date. Her stomach had tied itself in knots, just as it was now. Through her mad dash from the porch to the front door, she'd marveled — *I wonder if this man will be the father of my children? I wonder if this man will change my life forever?*

And now, she wondered something similar about Bruce.

Already, he'd changed everything.

She pulled open the front door to find him looking so handsome with his bright seafoam-green eyes locked with hers. In his hands, he held a bouquet of lilies.

"Hello there," he said finally. They were the simplest words in the world, yet they made Elsa's stomach flip back.

"Aren't you a sight for sore eyes?" Elsa said.

She took the flowers and felt her own face flourish with wonderment. Emotion was a marvelous and dangerous thing. Pain and pleasure and happiness and life, it was all connected. You couldn't have any of it without the others.

They held one another's gaze for a long time. The smell of sizzling burgers stretched out from the porch as Carmella called out.

"Well? Are you two going to get back here, or should I drink both of your margaritas for you?"

Elsa burst into giggles. She then stepped back to allow Bruce to enter. "I think you're going to really like my family," she told him as they stepped through the shadows and back toward the light of the porch. "They're a handful, but they're mine."

# Coming next in the Katama Bay Series

Read Summertime Nights

# Other Books by Katie

# Connect with Katie Winters

BookBub
Facebook
Newsletter

To receive exclusive updates from Katie Winters please sign up to be on her Newsletter!

CLICK HERE TO SUBSCRIBE

Ingram Content Group UK Ltd.
Milton Keynes UK
UKHW022146160623
423577UK00012B/970